Leah
Worlds Apart #1

By

Andrea Baker

ISBN: 9780992859312

2nd Edition

Published by: Rose Wall Publishing

For Jessica.

Wherever life takes us, we will always be together in our hearts.

To Chris and my family:

Without you I would never have started this journey, thank you for your love, patience and understanding.

Prologue

Sitting here, breathing in the familiar smell of wild flowers and sheltering under the huge old tree, I still found it difficult to comprehend everything that had happened. The air smelt slightly damp as though a storm was coming and I gave an involuntary shudder. Even now, knowing the truth, the fear of those storms had not completely dissipated. I leant my head back against the trunk, fitting nicely into the spot that I had occupied so many times before. Although I now knew I could do this at will, my stomach clenched with apprehension at what was to come. I knew that I would never want to revisit this period in my life again, I just needed to make sense of it this one final time. I just needed to be careful, to make sure I didn't change anything that had happened, otherwise there would be consequences.

Opening my laptop, I returned to the messages I had sent my best friend Jen. All I needed was a trigger, to place me in the right moment in time. As I started to read I smiled, remembering the friendship and familiarity of that time, before everything changed. Then I let myself start to float; drifting back, allowing myself to occupy my old body and thoughts, carefully and silently, avoiding anything that could bring the change to the attention of those around me.

Jen,

Well, we've finally unpacked – or I should say that I have! Dad's been at work most of the time, though I guess that doesn't surprise you. His behaviour is still off – I'd really hoped it would improve once we got away from the old house and the constant reminders. He's been going on about my needing a new start again – but after that last row, I just daren't argue with him anymore. His mood swings can be just so scary and the temper has definitely not improved – in fact if anything it is getting worse. So much for the fresh start he banged on about!

How's Aber? I am SO jealous. Bet the sun's shining isn't it? Where's your room, is it facing the sea, or the mountains? Still wish I could have come with you, like we'd always planned but I lost that argument the day Mom died…

Still Warwick should be ok, it's got a good reputation and the course seemed just right, so need to keep my focus on that now, not worry about what could have been.

Anyhow, this place is ok really – even though it's very old. Kenilworth town itself is a bit old school but you should see the Castle. I love it up there. I can take my music and wander around for hours, or if the weather's good I can just snuggle into a corner and read. No-one bothers me and it's SO Goth – you'd love it. I looked it up on Google and apparently there are parts of it that date back as far as Norman times and it also played quite an important role in some siege. Some of it has been rebuilt, turned into offices, tea rooms (with the blue rinses to match LOL) but I like the ruins best. There's an old Abbey too, at the other end of town but there's not much of that left, with far too many kids playing in the park for me and it's not like I've got anyone to play tennis with here.

The cottage itself apparently dates back to the 17th Century and has some connection to Walter Raleigh and the potatoes. It has three little corridors leading off to different, really odd shaped rooms – some people would hate it but I don't and I know you won't either. It's easy to hide in the attic and pretend not to hear Dad. Can't wait 'til November when you come to stay – I'm going to hold you to that promise!

Has Freshers started there properly yet? I don't start for a few more weeks but I feel physically sick when I think about it. I'm not looking forward to being the new girl but I guess we have that in common.

At the moment though I've still got some time to myself – not that Dad likes THAT of course. I'm sure he thinks Greg will turn up out of the blue or something – as if! That boat sailed, back in Clifford and I don't ever want to see HIM again. Men are most definitely off the agenda and not just because of the promise Dad forced out of me. Wonder if that has something to do with these dreams I'm getting…

Can't wait to hear all your news, don't keep me waiting.

L

The Beginning

"_Leah, you have to listen to me, you're in real danger._"

I jumped, glancing towards the shadowy figure beside me.

I shook my head in confusion, how could anything here be dangerous? It felt so safe. I sensed his arm wrap around my shoulders, holding me tight against him, protecting me.

There was a nagging voice in my head telling me not to be stupid, who **was** this person and what gave **him** the right to tell me what to do, let alone touch me like this?

As though in defiance of these thoughts I felt myself respond to his touch, in a way I'd never felt before. Instinctively I responded to his touch, feeling compelled to snuggle in even closer. I didn't move, unable to pull myself away but at the same time angry with myself for not moving away from this stranger.

The noise grew closer; I still couldn't quite work out what it was. It was loud... persistent... a *kind of roar. It was so loud that I couldn't make out where it was coming from. We don't have wild animals like wolves or bears around here anymore and it didn't really sound like an animal anyway. There wasn't that much life to it...*

His arm suddenly tightened around me. The sensation spread throughout my body, warming me as it went. Despite the noise and everything else, I felt as though I could stay here forever.

Suddenly a car pulled alongside us. "Get in!" screamed the driver. I flinched, not expecting to hear **that** *voice, not now. He grabbed my arm and before I knew it we were in the back of the car and he was struggling to get my seatbelt on. I snatched it off him as he dived into the seat beside me. "Go!" he yelled. The car accelerated away, filling with the scorching smell of burnt rubber. Where was I and who* **were** *these faceless people? He turned towards me but his face hidden by the shadows. With both of his hands on my shoulders, he pulled me in close to him.*

"Thank God you're safe," he said, burying his head in my hair. Without any conscious thoughts, my body

relaxed and all of a sudden the last thing I wanted was to be alone.

Abruptly, there was a huge crash from somewhere right alongside the car. "Step on it!" he bellowed, reaching across me to grab something...

"Leah, Leah! It's ok! Sweetheart, wake up."

Reluctantly I dragged myself away from those safe arms, as Dad gently shook me awake. I opened my eyes and looked up as his face hovered into view next to me. In the haze of sleep, just for a split second, there was something not quite right about his eyes; they looked bizarre, almost devoid of anything. Then, as I focussed on him, he smiled gently,

"Another one of those bad dreams?" he asked, gently rubbing my back. "Tell me about it?" he asked.

The stranger's voice echoed again in my head: "tell no-one!"

I shook the sleep from my thoughts and smiled weakly up at his face. "Just the usual, nothing new this time," I replied, already feeling guilty as I glanced at the clock by my bed. Why did I feel the need to keep the details of the dreams from my Dad? After all, it **was** only a dream…

Still, I didn't want Dad to worry. He had enough on his plate and he needed to believe that moving away had been the right thing to do for us both. Even though I had already realised that the dreams had become significantly worse since we had come here.

"Just give me a minute Dad and I'll go and make us both a coffee." I tried to hide the resentment in my tone, this was just one of the jobs I'd had to pick up over the last five years and even though the nightmares wouldn't allow a lie-in, sometimes it would have been nice for Dad to make me the coffee first thing in the morning.

He smiled at me softly for a few brief seconds before ambling away. A few moments later I heard his bathroom door close. I lay there for a moment trying to piece together the face from my dream and recalling the feeling from when the stranger had held me. Shaking myself, hard, I laughed. I'd promised my Dad to steer clear of boys after the break up with Greg and it felt like a betrayal even thinking about some man in my dreams. Besides, that sensation had been nothing like I'd felt when I was with Greg.

Swiftly, I went downstairs to start breakfast and put the coffee on. As it started to gurgle, the smell began to permeate the kitchen and I heard Dad coming downstairs. Anxiously I rammed my book and sandwiches into my bag and went to pour the coffee, shaking the vitamin bottle loudly, so that Dad would believe I had taken them.

"What are your plans for today then?" he said as he came into the kitchen, eyeing the thermal cup I was also filling. He nodded with satisfaction as he saw me replace the vitamins on the shelf. It was so bizarre how obsessed he was with making sure I took one of them every single day – it wasn't as if I needed them. As I did all of the cooking these days, I made sure we both had a properly balanced diet; after all we only had each other now.

Instinctively I tensed. "I thought I would go for a walk up to the castle and explore for a bit," I responded, nervously waiting for him to react.

He looked at me sideways. I didn't need him to remind me that he didn't like me wandering around up there on my own; neither did I want another one of his lectures or for him to lose his temper again.

"It'll be fine Dad, honest, there are so many tourists around with the good weather, it's not like I'll really be on my own." I tried to reassure him before his temper had time to build. What on earth could happen to me anyway in this sleepy little town? There was far more danger from my own home and in my dreams.

Dad drank his coffee and quickly ate the toast that I had prepared for us both. He kissed my forehead, already preoccupied with thoughts of work and left the house. I sighed with relief; the normal lecture had been avoided. Dad had a real issue with my being on my own, especially here in this new town and around the ruins.

I loaded the cups and plates into the dishwasher and switched it on making sure that everything was ready for dinner later – yet another chore I had picked up. Checking I had my phone and keys, I picked up my bag and left the house. It was still quite early and it was only a ten minute walk up to the Castle. I preferred to enter it from the Mortimer's Tower, even though the path by Leicester's Gatehouse and the Stable was probably a little closer. They were part of the renovated area, so were often busier. It was strange though seeing the fresh terracotta stone on such an old building. I guess that the whole place had been that colour when it was built and they had simply cleaned these parts during the renovations. Once you had got past the ticket office and down the long path, you could turn left at Mortimer's Tower and soon be away from the tourists.

Dad said that he found it morbid there. There were decent rambling walks around the grounds and across into the fields but it was the ruins I loved the most. They'd tried to make it attractive, with the renovation and the new Victorian Garden but there was a lot just left as nature intended and this was exactly what drew me to it. Despite the renovations, the oldest part of the castle, with its huge lumps of brick, blackened by time and surrounded by the beautiful Warwickshire countryside seemed eternally peaceful. The fields seemed to go on for miles on this side of the grounds.

Wandering around the ruins listening to my music, or simply sitting and reading in the quiet, I felt safer here than anywhere else. I'd lean back against the walls and imagine Mom was here with me. I'd tell her everything – my worries, my insecurities and my fear about Dad and his temper. In my mind she would answer, making sense of it all and helping me get some perspective back

Dad thought it was odd that this was where I liked to spend my spare time. I hadn't told him about feeling closer to Mom, that would have sent him off the rails. He'd never understood my desire to be on my own for long periods of time, so I left it like that. Explanations could be difficult.

***

I was out of breath by the time I reached the top of the hill. My spirits rose when I saw that the car parks and pathways were still relatively deserted, only old Bill and his retriever could be seen. That meant I had the opportunity to find my spot and settle in before the tourists arrived. I wondered idly if this town was always full of them, or if it was due to the unusually warm summer that we were having.

I wandered through the ruins, smiling to myself as I took in the smell of the newly cut grass and the wild flowers, which continually defied any attempt at cultivating the area. It was so beautiful here but it should be left wild, that was how it was meant to be, after all these years of belonging only to the elements.

I turned the corner and sighed with contentment; my favourite spot was right here, to the back of the Great Hall, amongst the longer grass and flowers and it was still deserted. I snuggled into the corner, leaning comfortably against the corners of the ruined walls, the long grass making a wonderfully soft aromatic cushion beneath me. I shuffled backwards until the wall bore most of my weight and put my head back, letting the morning summer sun warm my skin.

I closed my eyes, allowing my thoughts to wander. There were just a few weeks left until the term started and I had carefully chosen my new clothes. The University didn't have a real uniform of course, not like my old school but I knew it was still important to fit in. When I hadn't been idling away my time around the ruins, I'd carefully watched and analysed what the other local kids were wearing. My wardrobe for the new term now consisted of the standard items that most of the girls seemed to wear, several pairs of denim, baggy jumpers and shirts, boots and trainers. I ran through my choices in my mind , that should help keep me relatively anonymous, the last thing I wanted was to stand out, or make a fool of myself like I had that day I'd tried to dress up for Greg...

There was that sound again. It sounded as though it was right on top of me. What the hell was it? My unconscious mind searched for an answer. There was something innately familiar, scarily so but I still couldn't place it. I felt my heart begin to race as that same voice shouted to me.

"Come with me Leah, now!"

The snap of a twig made me start with fright. Shakily I looked up at the shadow standing to the side of me. The sun behind it made it impossible to make out who it was and besides, I still didn't know anyone from around here.

"Is everything ok?"

The voice brought me back to my senses. I must have dozed off in the warmth of the sun but the dreams had never occurred away from home before…

Squinting in the sunlight, I shaded my eyes trying to make out the figure standing over me. Every nerve in my body was suddenly on edge.

"Sorry, I really didn't mean to startle you. Here, let me help you. I'm Ben." He put his hand out to help me up but I ignored the offer, still more than a little shaken.

Scrambling up, I walked around to his side, so that I could see the stranger more clearly. For some reason it felt important for me to also establish myself as being in control of the situation, despite this unwanted interruption. Feeling that I had made the point, I breathed an inward sigh of relief and started to calm down a little, even though my heart was still pounding. The stranger was a young man, appearing to be roughly the same age as me. I turned fully towards him, trying to see him properly now that the sun wasn't in my eyes. Immediately I was struck by his height; he must be at least 6ft, as he seemed taller than Greg had been when standing next to me. The morning sun revealed the slightest hint of red in his wavy brown hair and the glint in his striking blue eyes somehow encouraged me to smile in return. Tearing my eyes away from his face, I noticed that he was wearing the type of understated jeans and t-shirt that didn't come cheap. As I registered more of his appearance, I felt the heat start to rush to my face and forced myself to look away. Normally, I didn't react to a boy in this way, or certainly hadn't before, even with Greg but there was definitely something about him. I'd even go as far as to say he was totally hot. The heat burned brighter in my cheeks as I struggled to compose myself, I didn't know Ben and after all I had a promise to keep.

"Hi, I'm Leah," I said awkwardly, starting to wonder why I had felt quite so annoyed, after all he had only tried to help. Now that I had the chance to look at him properly and register his age, I realised he would probably be going to the University too. I desperately wanted not to be on my own that first day and Ben was likely to be my best chance to avoid that.

"Seriously, *are* you ok?" he asked, the concern in his voice evident.

"Yes, of course... why?" I asked, confused, both by his show of genuine concern and the light-headedness that I guess still lingered from jumping up so quickly.

"I thought I heard a really strange noise and came to check everything was ok, but there's only you here," he replied.

"It was probably just my snoring. I fell asleep in the sun," I joked, suddenly anxious to get away. I didn't want to have to try and explain anything to a complete stranger, let alone my dreams – I couldn't even talk about those with my own Dad.

He laughed and the warmth of the sound made me start to relax again. He wasn't some freak about to jump me. Just a nice guy thinking he had heard something – most people would have just ignored it, rather than coming to check everything was ok.

"Look, do you fancy a coffee or something?" It came blurting out and suddenly he looked really self-conscious, as though he regretted being quite so bold and a pink tinge coloured his cheeks. Not having the heart to embarrass him, I agreed and picked up my bag, checking everything was in there. The fifteen minute walk to the coffee shop flew by as we talked – I discovered that his family had lived in this area for generations and he had a younger sister. Most importantly for me, he was starting at the University next month too.

"I haven't seen you around here before have I?" he asked once we were seated with our drinks. The smell of roasted coffee wafted around us as we talked, with the occasional breath of vanilla or mocha, as other people walked by.

I explained that Dad and I had moved earlier this month from a little village in Hertfordshire, because of my starting University, although it was mainly due to the relocation of Dad's job. The explanation seemed to satisfy him but I didn't elaborate about Mom, other than explaining she had died; it was always hard, having to explain. Thankfully he didn't pry and diverted the topic away to our impending studies. I was planning to read Business Studies with Marketing, while Ben explained that he would be doing Physical Sciences, so it was immediately obvious that we wouldn't be in any of the same classes. As the time passed, we talked about what we were hoping to choose as our first year supplementary courses and the all important clubs to be chosen during Freshers Week at the University. Before I knew it the rest of the day had flown by and the coffee shop was turning quiet.

I glanced at my watch. "I'm sorry," I muttered, suddenly really anxious, "I really need to go. Dad will expect me to be there when he gets home." It was a good twenty minute walk back to the cottage and Dad would be home at just about the same time, he would be furious if dinner wasn't almost ready when he arrived.

"Here, why not let me give you a lift?" Ben said, noticing my concern. "It's more or less on the way and it is partly my fault that you've been out all day." He smiled and I felt a strange flutter in the pit of my stomach.

Concerned about the time and despite my normal reluctance to accept such an offer from someone I barely knew, I agreed gratefully and we walked quickly to his car. I'm no expert when it comes to cars but I knew this one, it was a Mini John Cooper. The boys back at my old school had all longed for one of these; pictures of the various options had been plastered all over the sixth form common room walls. It had obviously been customised but the British Racing Green was unmistakable. The growl that came from the engine indicated the power the car had and we quickly sped along the road home.

"Do you think we could meet up again before term starts?" he asked as I clambered out. I turned back, surprised. "You're not the only one who's going to be new to the University and it would be nice to have a familiar face to walk in with on Day 1," he smiled, looking a little sheepish. Feeling awkward and also guilty, I agreed to meet him for coffee a couple of days later, then said goodbye and rushed into the cottage.

***

Suddenly grateful for my normally organised state, I started to throw the salad into the bowl, filling the kitchen with the smell of fresh onion and lettuce. Despite the activity, my mind started ranting again at the unfairness of it all. How many other nineteen year olds were confined to domestic routines like this? It was hardly my fault that Mom was gone, yet it felt as though I was the one being punished by her absence, while Dad's life continued as normal. Shaking my head in frustration I continued to finish the food preparation. Dad got home just as I was placing the saucepan onto the hob and I was instantly ready to cook the pasta, leaving him none the wiser to what I'd been up to.

"How'd your day go?" he asked as we sat down to dinner.

"Not bad," I replied, "I met another newbie in town, we're going to meet for coffee on Thursday."

"That's nice," he said, reading the paper as we talked, paying very little attention as usual. Although annoyed at his lack of interest in my life, I was also glad he didn't ask too many questions. I can't begin to explain why but somehow I didn't want to have to elaborate on how Ben and I had met and what we had been talking about today. Besides, his temper would flare if he thought I had been talking to a person of the opposite sex...

Eyes

"Leah, listen to me, please, we must get out of here right now!"

There it was again, that warm, gentle voice, warning me of some kind of danger. It was interrupted by that equally familiar but far more disturbing growl. This time it sounded much closer, although I still couldn't make out what it was.

The same car squealed to a halt, with my senses assaulted by the scorched rubber and again that oh-so familiar voice yelled at us to jump in. This time I was dragged in and held tightly as the person next to me cursed.

"Step on it!" he shouted. A thud from behind made us both jump and I spun to look out of the rear view window. Directly level with my own, a pair of luminous yellow eyes stared at me from shadows at the back of the car.

***

I woke abruptly, disorientated from my dream, looking around my room. From the doorway, that same pair of yellow eyes were watching me closely, completely motionless and devoid of life...

I sat bolt upright, grabbing the bedside lamp switch as I did so, then laughed at myself as it illuminated the room. It was just another dream, of course, there was nothing there.

When my breathing had quietened enough that I could stand without my legs buckling, I left my bedroom and padded softly downstairs and into the kitchen. These dreams had been getting so much worse since we'd moved. I'd had bad dreams for as long as I could remember but none quite as frequent, or as consistent as this. I gingerly sipped the cocoa I'd made as I made my way through to the lounge. I couldn't stop thinking about the dreams and wondering what they meant. With the kind of rationality that comes in the very early morning, I came to the conclusion that it was my subconscious worrying about the move and starting at the University. I wondered which one of my new classmates would have the weird yellow eyes and chuckling to myself I climbed back upstairs, hoping to be able to get some more sleep before Dad woke up and I had to tell him yet again about another bad dream. What was the point in worrying him about it?

A few hours later, I awoke to the bright morning light coming through my bedroom window. For a brief second I was completely disorientated, it was the first time in quite a while that I had woken up properly without the jolt of my bad dreams. As my brain clicked into action, the memory of the night before crept in and I laughed at myself, convinced that I had finally identified the cause behind this latest bout of nightmares and therefore rid myself of them completely. I'd had similar nightmares in the past but Mom had always talked them out with me, so they disappeared after a few days. This time they had seemed to go on for many months and had become much worse since the move. Pleased with myself, I stretched, feeling more rested then I had for a very long time and then glanced at the clock. As I did, I cringed. By the faint whiff of cold toast and old coffee, I could tell that Dad was long gone and he would be furious that I hadn't made breakfast. As it was I only just had time to get ready before I was due to meet Ben at the coffee shop. The image from last night popped into my brain and despite myself I looked towards the doorway of my room, unable to quell the sense of trepidation as I did so. I laughed out loud, of course there was nothing there...

For a brief second I played with the idea of crying off from meeting Ben and then realised I had no way of actually letting him know. Despite not particularly wanting to go and appearing to be desperate to see him again, I still didn't like the idea of standing him up, Ben deserved better than that. Reluctantly I climbed out of bed and started to get ready.

As I dried off after my shower I winced and was surprised to notice a large purple bruise across the top of my arm. For a few moments I racked my brain trying to remember how I had hurt myself. I guessed that I must have caught the door or something last night when half asleep and shrugging my shoulders I rushed through the final stages of getting ready. After a last quick check in the mirror I ran for the door and left, with only seconds to spare.

I shivered suddenly and glanced up at the sky. It was considerably cooler today than it had been recently and the breeze smelt as though it was bringing a storm with it. I hated storms, they genuinely frightened me – it had been a particularly vicious storm the day that Mom had died and even though I hadn't been with her at the time, they had made me nervous ever since.

As I walked down High Street, I scolded myself for allowing someone to corner me like this. I had absolutely no idea who Ben really was, so why had I agreed to meet him in this way? I certainly didn't want to get involved with anyone right now and there was also my promise to keep. Meeting him like this was bound to give the wrong impression. Briefly I pictured him in my mind again, not that I'd have any objection to being involved with him…

"Get a grip girl," I suddenly laughed to myself. It was a huge assumption that Ben was even interested in me in that way, let alone worrying about getting involved. I was certainly no catch, the boys at my last school had shown little interest and as Greg had pointed out when we broke up; I was particularly boring in the looks department. So why would Ben be any different. He was probably just being polite and as he had said, wanting a friendly face for the first day until he got to know the other new students and then he too would probably ditch me at the first opportunity.

With that thought now straight in my mind, I walked into the coffee shop. I spotted Ben quite easily, as the place was relatively quiet at this hour. As I sat down, I noticed a guitar case next to him on the seat.

"Do you play?" I asked.

"A little," he replied, almost bashfully. "I'm in a band, called Liberation. We play at one or two of the local bars and sometimes at the Student's Union. One of the other band members is in his final year there already. This is Lady Bess," he admitted sheepishly as he lightly patted the case.

"Are you any good?" I asked, surprised; this didn't fit my perception of him at all.

"Not bad I suppose, or so we are told. Why don't you come see for yourself, we're rehearsing up at the University later on? They let us use the practise rooms, as it is outside of term and at least one of us is officially a student – technically I don't become a student until the start of term and then there will be two of us," he offered.

"Maybe."

I hesitated. I'd fully intended to wander off to the ruins again this afternoon after I'd left him and had already plotted a couple of excuses to escape him if he tried to hang about – but the idea of actually getting to see inside University early, without the crowds of people so that I could get a proper feel for the place, was really tempting.

Just as I was debating with myself whether to accept, or stick to my original plan, the weather decided for me. Our conversation was interrupted by a sudden flash of lightning, followed almost immediately with one of the loudest rumbles of thunder I had ever heard. I almost shot out of my chair with the noise.

Ben laughed. He had been caught by surprise just as I had but he was laughing at me – in my shock I had managed to spill my coffee all over the table when I flinched and it was only his laughter that made me realise what had happened and this prevented the scalding liquid spilling over onto my legs. I jumped up, mortified. My face must have been the colour of beetroot. I quickly grabbed some napkins and started to mop up the mess, apologising as I did so –especially when I realised it had ran over some papers he had in front of him, that were obviously to do with his music.

"Don't worry," he insisted, "I know them all by heart anyway, I just use these for appearances sake."

I knew he was just being kind and hid my face behind my hair as I concentrated on trying to clean up the mess. As I did so, thunder erupted again but this time without the disastrous results indoors. I was so intent on avoiding looking at him, I only realised he'd left the table when he placed another coffee in front of me.

"Thanks," I mumbled, hugely embarrassed. I looked up sheepishly, to meet the humour still residing in his blue eyes. For a split second I felt as though I could drown right there and then. Noting my continued anguish he tried to straighten his face and changed the subject, just as the thunder erupted yet again. I looked up startled, this storm did not seem to be moving on at all and each flash of lightning seemed just as close as the last.

"Come on, why don't you come hear us practise, it's got to be better than walking around in the rain," he said, a hopeful look on his face. To be honest, he was right – what else was I going to do in this storm, other than get soaked on the way home and then spend the day moping around the cottage? It was too wet even to escape in our back garden. For lack of a better alternative, I agreed.

The thunder didn't seem to be letting up at all, so Ben ran to get the car, leaving me with Lady Bess and his music. A few moments later he pulled up out

front, I threw everything into the back seat and
jumped in, grateful to be out of the rain.

***

I'd never realised before how long it took to set
up a band rehearsal. It was quickly apparent why it
was so useful for them to be able to practise here; it
seemed that the room contained everything they
needed except for their own instruments. Ben tried to
explain the difference between the amps and the PA
system but it went straight over my head. The
banging and scraping of the equipment as they
shifted it and the brash sounds of tuning guitars
quickly got boring, so making an excuse I wandered
out into the corridor and across to the large window.
I hadn't realised until we got here just how close
some of the campus was to Dad's work and I'd been
relieved to find the Faculty of Music was on one of
the satellite sites on the opposite side of the main
campus. Although I could see Gibbet Hill from this
window, it was unlikely that Dad would see me
anywhere near here, or in the car with Ben. I jumped

as an old rasping voice interrupted my thoughts and I spun around to see wise old brown eyes, inside a weather beaten face and faded blue overalls on a bent wiry body. Before I could speak however the stranger had turned the corner and the sound of music started to escape from the room that I had left.

I was the only spectator to the practise. The other guys seemed ok with me being there and to be honest once they started playing they were more or less oblivious to my presence, which suited me fine. Although I was reluctant to admit it, I was surprised to find that weren't half bad.

As they ran through a combination of covers that I knew and instrumental music that I had never heard before, I found myself enjoying the session. Although I like music, I'd never really paid much attention to the local scenes, especially here in the new town. I couldn't help wondering whether they played to a local fan base and had their own groupies, or whether they just hid away and practised like this, limiting themselves to vacant rooms and small locals, where nobody actually listened. Suddenly I was hoping that was not the case.

It was interesting watching Ben with his friends. Although he had seemed quite tall when we first met, it seemed less obvious when he was with his friends but he still stood out as being the most attractive of the three. Wickedly I remembered how sensitive Greg had been about his lack of height and how much it would annoy him if I were to point that out; I would have loved him to see me here, now with these three tall, good looking men. Ben introduced me to Will first. He was the bass player and standing next to the others his pale skin and sandy hair stood out against the others' mellower colours. Rich, who played the rhythm guitar, was the shortest of the three men, although there only seemed to be an inch or so between them. He didn't say very much but his blond curls bounced as they played and his pale blue eyes sparkled with pleasure.

At some point during the session the thunder subsided. Ben ran me home afterward and we agreed to catch up again the day after tomorrow.

Shopping

I lay in bed that night, thinking about the events of the day. I'd really enjoyed listening to the band play, particularly the instrumental stuff, which had never really appealed to me before. As I relaxed, I started humming one of the pieces quietly. Ben had offered to pick me up a few days later and I was planning to ask him if he had a copy that I could put onto my iPod.

There was that awful sound again. This time I was already in the car. Slowly, fearfully, I turned around to look at the boot – those incandescent yellow eyes were there again, staring ferociously at me. I cringed and turned back, in time to see the shadow man throwing something through the open window. It hadn't looked like a weapon, although judging by the howl that came from the side of the road it did the job of one. I wondered what he had aimed at and why he hadn't gone for the thing hanging on to the back of the car.

I didn't have time to think too much though. Suddenly the car was swerving around a bend and

despite the seatbelt, I found myself thrown almost
into his lap. I pushed myself away, trying desperately
to get a look at his face but it was always in the
shadows.

There was another crash and suddenly the
yellow eyes were at the car window. I found myself
trying to hide in the seat of the car, pushing as far
away from the window as I could. The eyes continued
to stare at me for what seemed like an age.

I opened my eyes and lay there in the half
darkness. I could feel my heart racing from the dream
but at least I had somehow managed to not wake Dad
up again this time and for that I was grateful. I
couldn't understand why the dreams continued and
were even getting worse, despite my reasoning about
the cause. It wasn't as if I was starting university
without knowing anyone, now I'd met Ben.

At what seemed like exactly the same moment
to that thought, the skies erupted again and my
stomach started to churn with my usual reaction to an
impending storm. The wind had picked up

considerably but now it appeared to drop and with the stillness came yet another storm. I jumped up and pushed my window closed. I normally slept with the window partially locked open but I didn't want the rain coming in.

I curled up on my bed and flicked the reading light on. I lay there thinking. It was times like this that I really missed having Mom to talk to. We would have been able to talk about these dreams properly. Somehow with Dad it always seemed harder. Don't get me wrong, he tries really hard but it just isn't the same. Mom and I were always close, so close it almost seemed as though we could read each other's minds, often answering questions before they were even asked. What had happened still didn't make sense to me, nor did the fact that at times it felt as though we were still having conversations in the same way.

I shook myself, no point thinking about that now. I turned the light off and lay there listening to the storm. Hoping that it would die away quickly and then dry up before morning, so I could still visit the ruins. Listening to the rain pounding outside though, that seemed unlikely.

I must have dozed off again however, as when I awoke the rain had stopped. I still couldn't shake that uneasy feeling as I showered and got dressed for the day. As I looked outside, I resigned myself to the fact that it was going to be too wet to visit the ruins again today and put my mind to planning what to do, rather than mope around the cottage all day. I thought of yesterday's music session and smiled. The guys in the band had all been pretty good about my attendance, although I had caught a look passing between Richard and Will that had intrigued me. I wasn't likely to find out what it meant though until I got to know them better. I smiled to myself, I was hardly your usual music fan – I recognised the tunes but it was very rare that I could give you the title or even the name of the artist. Ben **was** nice, I had to admit that and not just in the way he looked. What was important was that he was gentle and interested in me as a person, unlike Greg, who had wanted me simply as another conquest to mock and make me look bad. Ben was not like the boys back in Clifford, he was different, not that he would be interested in the likes of me anyway.

Other than Greg, I hadn't really had a proper boyfriend before and after the way Greg had treated me, I didn't want to have one either. There had been the occasional "date" to see a film but these had usually taken place in small groups, or at least with another couple and I'd never really clicked with anyone enough to want to see them as just the two of us. Not that anyone had shown a particular interest in me either. There had been Joe, who I'd more or less grown up with back home. He had once told me he'd got tickets to see a gig but didn't have anyone to go with – but that didn't count as an invitation did it?

Not that Ben would be interested in me like that anyway, he was only being civil, I was sure of that. Although he said he was new at the University too, he had said that his family had lived here for generations, so he obviously wasn't new to the entire area, otherwise where did Liberation fit in?

I looked at myself in the mirror as I finished getting ready. The light in this old cottage wouldn't do anyone any favours but then it would take a miracle to do something for me. I'd never really had that much interest in my appearance. Like all girls of that age, I'd started to get interested in clothes and things before Mom died but afterwards, there was no-one to offer help or advice. Dad had been pretty useless with anything like that.

I stared at my reflection, wondering if there was anything I could do to improve on my appearance right now. Unbidden, the memory of the last time I'd try to do anything like that crept into my mind. Greg and I had been going out together for a few weeks and he'd asked me to go to the Christmas party with him. Wanting to make him proud of me, I'd spent all day curling my lifeless hair and practising with makeup. I'd been quite proud of the result and even Dad had grunted his approval. I'd entered the room with pride, holding my head up high for once, certain that Greg would be delighted in what he saw. Even now, months later, I shivered at the memory of the reaction that I'd got. He'd roared with laughter from the other side of the room, shouting at his mates to look and calling me a clown. Before I knew it the whole room seemed to be pointing and laughing and I turned and ran, out into the snow and ice, falling down the steps and ripping my new skirt in the process.

Tears welled at the memory of the humiliation. Angry for allowing it to still hurt; I rinsed my face in cold water and then looked again in the mirror. Boring would be the best description for what I saw. Green/brown hazel eyes, dirty blonde hair, average height and average build. The perfect mediocre appearance for someone that no-one wanted to notice, or needed to remember.

I looked outside, although the rain had stopped, the wind had picked up again and the whole place looked grey and damp. I decided to walk into town and see what the shops had to offer, or not as was probably the case. Still, I could always catch the bus into Leamington Spa if need be, anything to get out of the cottage and away from my thoughts and dreams.

As I was about to leave, I thought again of yesterday's music and an idea struck me. I quickly booted up my computer and searched online for a band called Liberation. As I thought, there were no downloadable tracks listed. No luck there then.

I walked slowly into town, shoulders hunched against the damp conditions. It was a good job I was used to this kind of weather, someone less hardy would have hated the place at the moment. I smiled as I walked – Mom would have hated the town, it was too claustrophobic. Unlike me, she would not have ventured out to the ruins to find space and solitude.

Just as I arrived in the square, the Leamington Spa bus was turning the corner. On the spur of the moment I decided to jump on, rather than waste time around town and then have to wait for the next bus. I started to run for the stop but the driver just laughed and drove off. His excuse would be that no-one was waiting at the stop. I shook my head in frustration and was just about to turn back towards the high street when I heard a car horn. Looking back, I saw Ben waving out of the driver's window at me. Sheepishly, I smiled back. Nothing like making a fool of myself was there? I hesitated as he swung the car expertly into the space.

"Need a lift?" he asked, grinning.

"Not really, just thought I would try shopping in Leamington Spa for more choice but the driver obviously had other ideas," I replied. I couldn't help but smile back, despite my embarrassment.

"Jump in and I'll drop you off, I'm going that way anyhow," he said. A little reluctantly, I walked around the car and climbed in.

This time it was a more leisurely drive and I noticed a few times how people turned towards us as the car drove passed. At first I thought it was the sound of the car, that unusually low rumble that came from the engine. I wanted to ask about that but knew that I would make an even bigger fool of myself trying to sound like I knew anything about cars.

After a while, it dawned on me that it wasn't the car people were looking at, they were looking into the car and of course they must be looking at Ben. I looked at him out of the corner of my eye, trying to work out what was drawing their attention. I watched him for a while and came to the conclusion it was a combination of things. Whilst no-one would deny that he was very good looking and obviously kept himself in shape, there was far more to him than just his looks. The way he held himself, his build, his clothes, they all exuded a kind of presence. Far from showy, he was simply comfortable in his own skin. Well built, yes, "fit" as the other kids would say but there was an air of honesty and trust about him. There wasn't an ounce of conceit. He simply radiated the presence of someone that cared little about the trappings. He wasn't at all the sort that I would normally be attracted to but there was something, something that drew me to him and gave me a dull ache in the pit of my stomach. Suddenly he spoke:

"What's the verdict then, I know you've been scrutinizing me and weighing something up for the last couple of miles."

I flushed. I'd thought I was being discreet. Words escaped me for a short time, until he glanced my way and smiled gently.

"Come on, tell me," he said.

"I was trying to work out what people were looking at," I replied, having finally decided that honesty was the only approach here, as was normally the case.

"What makes you assume they are looking at me?" he smiled, then shrugged. "It has happened once before but I think then it was most likely the car – it was brand new at the time, although obviously today, there is **you**."

I looked away, completely self-conscious now, shaking my head. "They are most definitely looking on your side of the car," I replied. He looked back at me quickly, raising one eyebrow and then turned back to the road.

Desperate to change the subject, I looked around me, suddenly more than a little concerned.

"Where are we going? This isn't the way to Leamington Spa," I demanded, concern making my voice sound aggressive.

He glanced back at me. "If you want decent shops, you have to go a bit further afield. Don't worry; you won't be stuck with me all day. I'll drop you off and then meet you again later. I've got another appointment to keep."

The way he said that told me he wanted no more questions. I sat there quietly, suddenly nervous. What did I know about this guy really and now I was stuck in a car with him, going goodness knows where.

He must have sensed my concern, because he reached across the car and placed his hand on my arm. "Don't worry, **I'm** not one of the bad guys," he smiled, "I just thought you might appreciate a decent choice of shop – isn't that what you girls prefer?" he chuckled, "Or so I've been told."

I thought it strange that he said it like that but didn't want to pry, I felt too stupid and vulnerable. I resolved to find my own way home from wherever it was we were going. I looked down at his hand, still resting lightly on my arm, something felt comfortable, even vaguely familiar about his touch, as though it belonged there. Ben caught me looking and removed his hand slowly. Was I imagining the reluctance?

"Here we go," he said pulling into a bay. "A nice new shopping centre for you. I'll meet you on the first floor at one pm, in "La Tasca" for lunch and then I'll give you a ride back home." He turned to me, a warm smile on his face.

"Honestly Leah, you don't need to worry, you are completely safe with me, I promise. And just to prove it, why don't you ring and leave a message for your Dad saying where you are? You could even give him my car registration, so he can track me down if you fail to come home on time?"

He grinned as he went to hand me his cell phone and I got a funny feeling in the pit of my stomach: how did he know what I had been thinking? Embarrassed at being caught out once again I smiled and shook my head.

"I think enough people saw you on the way here to be able to report it if I end up missing," I replied, kicking myself for being so suspicious. When would I learn to stop judging everyone by the headlines in the newspapers?

Ben threw me a funny look but before I could question him further, he drove off. I turned and looked at the centre in front of me. He was right. This promised a much better choice of shops than either Kenilworth itself, or Leamington Spa. I wandered inside, trying to get my bearings. There was a Gap, Zara, Episode, John Lewis and Next – to name just those I could see from this entrance. There was also a book corner coffee stall and several wings leading off that could be explored. I wouldn't have too much difficulty in whiling away the time until lunch.

I decided first to find the restaurant, so I had my bearings for later. That done I went exploring. Ben was right, it was much better to have a choice, pity I didn't have that much money to spend. I enjoyed the window shopping though.

Before I knew it, it was time to meet up with Ben, so I made my way back to the restaurant, surprised to see that a queue had formed. There was no sign of Ben, so I decided to take a place in the queue. We could end up waiting for quite a while otherwise. Ben arrived when I was about halfway to the front and to my surprise, he walked straight to the front desk. Speaking softly to the waitress, she checked something in the book and then nodded and smiled up at him. He nodded his head in acknowledgment and then turned, scanning the faces before him. Suddenly his eyes rested on me and he smiled, beckoning me toward him. My stomach did a kind of flip-flop as I smiled back and then joined him at the front of the queue.

We were led to a table in a more private area of the restaurant. The waitress, still completely focussed on Ben, acted as though I didn't exist, which aggravated me more than a little. After we were seated and she'd left us with our menu, Ben finally noticed my irritated expression.

"What's the matter?" he asked, puzzled by the look on my face.

"How did you get seated in front of all of those people?" I demanded. He looked bewildered by my tone. "Well?" I repeated when he didn't answer.

He flushed and looked away from my accusing stare. "I always eat here when I have an appointment in the town," he replied, "so I had a reservation, I just needed them to make it a reservation for two, for a change." He still didn't meet my gaze, staring instead at the menu.

"What would you like?" he asked.

"I'm not that hungry," I replied, still fuming, although I couldn't work out quite why it had annoyed me so much. My stomach decided to betray me at that precise moment and growled. He met my gaze then, raising one eyebrow sarcastically. It was my turn to look away, as my stomach did that strange flip-flop again. I quickly scanned the lunchtime menu for something that would be quick and easy to eat, suddenly in a rush to get home.

To my frustration, Ben took it upon himself to order for both of us, the tapas selection for two. I had to admit that it sounded delicious but I was annoyed at his presumption that I would agree to that. Food ordered I suddenly felt flustered. Would he expect me to order an alcoholic drink? Whilst I was old enough to drink alcohol, I hadn't really had much experience with it, other than the odd glass of wine at a special meal and I wouldn't know what to ask for. To my relief and illogically, my annoyance, he ordered two glasses of sparkling water. The waitress flashed a brilliant smile at him, again ignoring my presence and I found myself glaring after her.

After she left, Ben looked at me apologetically.

"Sorry, that was very rude of me," he said. He looked shamefaced. "I should have asked you what you wanted but you are obviously upset about something and I could hear you were hungry," he smiled slightly, "so I went ahead and ordered so that you ate something at least. I can call the waitress back and change the order if you'd like," he added hurriedly.

I couldn't help but smile at his concern as my stomach did that peculiar little cartwheel again. "Don't worry, it made it easier – I'm not particularly good at Spanish, so I suppose it saved me the trouble of asking you to translate."

Despite my response, I still couldn't quite silence that little voice of annoyance in my brain but at least he had had the decency to apologise.

"The waitress wouldn't understand the problem anyway. As far as she was concerned you haven't got a companion today, so I am sure she would love **that** excuse to come back," I replied sarcastically. He raised those eyes to meet mine and my stomach turned again. At this rate I would be too motion sick to enjoy the food.

"Oh you don't need to worry about her," he smiled. "She's waited on me before and I left a decent tip because I had no change, so she is probably after the same again. Other than that I'm afraid bleached blondes really are not my type. However, awful as it sounds, it does come in useful when you want a quiet table!"

He looked around us as he spoke and my eyes followed his. Despite the queue outside, this part of the restaurant was pleasantly quiet, not too isolated but not sitting in each other's laps. Relaxing slightly, I became aware of the familiar music playing in the background.

"Hey, is this one of yours?" I asked, turning my head slightly to hear the sound better.

Ben looked surprised. "I wish but unfortunately not, you did hear us do a cover of it the other day though. Although I'm surprised you recognise it, our style is a little more laid back than this – you must have a very good ear."

We talked over lunch, about music mainly and the artists that had influenced him, from Hendrix to Joe Satriani as well as the likes of Mark Knopfler and

Eric Clapton, anything to do with guitars and rock melody, I soon realised.

Although not really something I knew that much about. I found myself enjoying the conversation, as he talked about the artists different styles and how he tried to incorporate them into his own work. Again I was struck by the thought that although obviously the same age as me, he somehow seemed different, or, at least more experienced, than I was.

Whilst I was pondering how to raise this without appearing rude, I noticed the weather again, yet another storm was brewing.

"This wind is terrible. So much for the mild summer we were having, I should have known it was too good to last."

Ben looked at me and nodded thoughtfully.

"We'd best be getting back soon, before your Dad gets home," he replied.

That little voice of annoyance piped up again as he settled the bill quickly, ignoring my attempts to pay my share, giving me that same bashful smile and then he led me through the centre to the car park. We talked all the way home, about a number of subjects, his music, films – all the things that I normally try to avoid in general conversation but somehow, this time, I didn't mind and the journey flew by. I was surprised when we arrived at the cottage to see that Dad was already home.

"Why don't you come in for a drink?" I asked, for some reason reluctant for this day to end. I couldn't remember the last time I had spent so long in someone else's company, without feeling pressurised to fit in. The knot in my stomach tightened knowing that Dad would not be impressed that I was back late.

"Best not to, I probably wouldn't be too welcome right now," Ben replied cryptically, glancing over at the cottage as he leant across me to open the door. "I'll see you tomorrow, as agreed?"

I watched him pull away, wondering what he had meant by his strange comment but as I turned towards the cottage I could see my Dad watching from the window. The look on his face mirrored the incessant stormy weather.

"Where the hell do you think you have been young lady?" he demanded as I let myself in. "And who was that you were with?"

I looked at him in surprise, I knew he had a volatile temper of course but he never usually reacted like this. Normally it was if I disagreed with him and it turned into an argument.

"That was Ben, I told you about him over dinner the day we met, he is starting the University soon too, so we will both be new starters," I replied, suddenly very uneasy.

"Well, **I** don't like you going off to strange places with **men** like that!" he stormed.

I stood silently, watching him stomp around our little kitchen, slamming pots down onto the stove and throwing the dirty preparation dishes into the sink. I struggled to understand why he was in such a mood, trying to rationalise it, when suddenly he practically flew across the kitchen, grabbed my arms, tight and started to shake me viciously.

"Don't you dare ever go off like that again!" he snarled. "Otherwise I will have no choice but to **make** you stay here!"

I pulled away from him in fear. How could he talk to me like that and what gave him the right to threaten me in such an aggressive way? I didn't move away quite quickly enough and turning back he pushed me violently towards the door, almost knocking me over with the force, before he stormed away once more. I could see him shaking but with what, rage? Fear? I really wasn't sure what the cause was but I wasn't going to hang around to find out. I turned and ran to my room slamming the kitchen door shut behind me.

I was past the legal age of independence and didn't have to live with him anymore, so there was no way he could force me to stay at home. Was there? As panic froze my mind, I tried to snap myself out of it but I just couldn't believe I was having these thoughts. Yes, he'd thrown things a few times and even slapped me before but never like this. The question of having to leave home, because of his temper had simply never occurred to me before.

I plugged my iPod into the speakers, putting the track on as loudly as possible, so that I didn't need to think. My arms still burned from where he had grabbed me.

What had that all been about? It really didn't make any sense. I quickly checked my phone – there weren't even any missed calls, so why had he flown off the handle like that at me? It wasn't as if he had been trying to track me down.

I refused to go downstairs for the rest of the evening and locked my door so that Dad couldn't come in, even if he had tried. I mooched around my room, reading, listening to music and watching my small, old fashioned TV with the original family DVD player. Anything to try to take my mind off what happened and the assortment of possible causes, I even wrote an email to Jen, explaining what had happened and how I felt – but I couldn't bring myself to send it. I didn't want anyone to know.

When I finally got ready for bed, my arm had an angry red handprint around it – you could even make out the shape of the fingers and nails. That was going to leave another nasty bruise, I thought. For the first time that summer, I found myself hoping that the weather stayed bad for tomorrow, so that I had an excuse to wear sleeves, the last thing I wanted to do was explain these particular marks to Ben.

Changing Dreams

I was dreading going to sleep that night, with what had just happened and the mood I was in, the nightmares were certain to be worse than ever.

I fought and fought against sleep, willing myself to stay awake, preferring exhaustion to the nightmares. Finally, at about three am, I finally drifted off, helpless against the anaesthetizing effects of sleep.

I was walking through the ruins, smiling to myself. It was a warm day and the air was filled with the scent of newly mown grass and wild flowers, so it must have been one from earlier that summer. I was having a mental conversation with Mom, telling her about the new cottage, the town and how I felt about the approaching new term. I could hear the smile in her voice as she replied:

"Don't worry Leah, I am with you each and every step of the way, you just need to think about me and I will be here, just as I always promised you."

Suddenly dusk was falling. The castle looked very different now and the evening lights, that normally lit the ruins from dusk until midnight, had failed. I turned the corner to my favourite spot and came to an abrupt halt.

There, standing in front of me, was a young girl. She couldn't have been any older than nine or ten. She had her back to me but from the way she was standing and her quivering movements, I could tell that she was crying.

"Hey, what's the matter, are you lost?" I called to her softly.

"I want my Daddy," came the quiet, tearful response.

"Where did you leave him?" I asked, walking towards her. "Come on, let's find our way back to the car park, I'm sure we will find him there and I bet he is worried sick about you." I smiled to myself, that had always been one of Mom's favourite sayings.

By this time I had reached her side and she looked up at me, tears streaming down her face. I held my hand out to take hers. She reached up to hold my hand but suddenly she was gone. The scene had shifted in an instant and now I was near to the occupied part of the castle, I could still hear the little girl crying for her Daddy but could not see her anywhere. I ran through the sectors that I knew so well, looking frantically everywhere. I was the only one who knew where this girl had been and her parents must be really worried by now.

The roar of the car engine brought me to a sudden stop. Where was it coming from? I turned quickly, eyes searching everywhere, cars weren't allowed in this part of the castle grounds. As I re - focussed, it dawned on me that the scene had changed again.

Suddenly I was back on the main road, opposite the castle entrance. The same black car screeched to a stop in front of me and I was again assaulted by the stench of scorched rubber. The door was thrown open. This time I didn't need to be told what to do, I was terrified.

I lunged into the car, pulling the door shut behind me. Where was my saviour now?

The car pulled away, picking up speed almost immediately, flying through the town that had become so familiar, I didn't want to think about what speed we were doing. I finally managed to get myself sitting up straight and reached for the seatbelt. As I did, I glanced at the rear view mirror towards the driver. Looking back at me was a pair of chilling yellow eyes. A flash of lightning illuminated the view, and for the first time I got a full view of the beast that had been haunting my dreams. Sinewy long legs with webbed feet held a hairless wiry body. As I watched, he dropped onto to all fours so that his eyes were level with mine, and my stomach plummeted as the realisation of the sheer size of this creature dawned on me. As if it read my thoughts it stood back onto those legs. Fully upright he was well over six foot tall. Claw-like hands that looked as powerful as his legs tore through the air as he raced after us, easily keeping pace with the car. Sharp pointed teeth grinned at me from his rounded face, and I realised the creature had not a single hair on his body. Opening his mouth wide, he uttered an ear-shattering yowl and I shuddered as thick, viscous saliva drooled from his bottom jaw.

I sat bolt upright in bed, heart hammering so loud I thought it would wake my Dad. I still hadn't forgiven him for last night, so the last thing I wanted was to be comforted by him. I didn't put the light on straight away; instead I stared out of my bedroom window at the stars. Surprisingly the sky had cleared while I slept. I lay there, listening to my heart hammer itself back to a normal rhythm.

I must have dozed back off, because suddenly there was that voice again.

"Trust me Leah; you will know what you need to do. Follow your own instincts and you will be fine, don't let others tell you what to do."

I twisted and turned, trying to identify where the voice was coming from but everything was black.

"I don't know what you mean. Please tell me, what do I need to do?" I begged, more confused than ever.

*"You'll know when the time comes, just follow your own instincts and **trust no-one.**"*

The voice and everything else for that matter, was gone and I was left with blissful nothingness.

I awoke slowly the next morning, unsure of what was happening, or where I was for that matter. The events of the previous evening and the dreams had left me bewildered and if I'm honest, scared. Trust my instincts – what a joke, I was so messed up that I wasn't sure anymore what day of the week it was.

I looked at the clock – good, Dad had most probably gone to work by now, although I would be in trouble again later for not having made his breakfast. Slowly I got out of bed, wincing. My arm really hurt now, much more than it had when I went to bed. Cautiously I took my arm out of my over-shirt. To my bewilderment, most of the upper part of

my arm was badly bruised, with Dad's fingerprints
still visible where he had seized me. It just didn't
make any sense at all. Although I was still really mad
with him for what had happened, which as far as I am
concerned was totally unjustifiable, there was no way
that he had hurt me this badly – and then there was
the mark on the other arm, which I still couldn't
explain. Was I getting sick?

My stomach sank at that thought – how would
I explain that to my Dad? He would find out that I
hadn't been taking my vitamins and there would be
hell to pay. Besides that, he had been through enough
with what had happened with Mom, I couldn't put
him through anymore. It wasn't as if I could go to the
Doctors with my concern right now either – the
newest injury was obviously from someone's hand
and angry as I was with him, I wasn't about to get
him embroiled in some kind of enquiry.

I went to the bathroom and rummaged through
the family "medicine box" – in reality a tatty old
Quality Street tin. I found a bandage and cooling
pack and with quite a bit of a struggle, finally

managed to wrap it around my upper arm. At least that helped with the pain when I moved my arm.

I glanced at the clock again. I was supposed to be meeting Ben again shortly, so I needed to hurry up. I glanced at myself in the bathroom mirror. The light in here never did me any favours but this morning it was worse than ever. If Ben had felt any inclination toward me before, he most definitely wouldn't by the time he saw me like this. For a split second I contemplated trying to conceal how bad I looked with make-up but soon disregarded that. I would end up looking worse than I did now and as I tended to only wear a little light eyeliner and lip gloss, it would raise more suspicions than it averted.

I got ready as quickly as I could, choosing a casual short sleeved shirt to wear over a t-shirt, in an attempt to hide the bandage. I grabbed my phone and bag and rushed downstairs.

There was no sign of Dad, he'd even cleared away his breakfast dishes before he left – I couldn't remember the last time he'd done that. It must be down to a sense of guilt for behaving like that last night I thought, with more than a glimmer of satisfaction. Despite that though, I was glad I didn't have to face him.

I hadn't looked outside in my rush to get ready – I did so as I opened the door. The sky was heavy and grey, it looked as though the good weather was gone completely now. Grabbing my umbrella, just in case, I started the walk toward the town centre.

After about half a mile, I suddenly heard a car horn. Turning, I immediately recognised Ben's car and couldn't help smiling back at him. I climbed in through the door he opened for me and he drove off as I secured the seatbelt, trying my hardest to hide the wince that the twisting movement brought about. As I turned back, I caught the end of a frown crossing his face but I decided it was best to ignore it, that way I wouldn't have to explain anything.

"I thought we could go for a coffee before we meet up with the rest of the band, if that is ok with you?" he asked. I was actually beginning to appreciate this more courteous side of him, rather than getting annoyed by him taking over.

"Sounds good to me, only this time I'll try not to spill it all over us both." We both laughed at the memory.

By the time we got to the coffee shop the heavens had opened again but this time the wind had increased too. It felt more like autumn than the middle of summer.

As we walked in, I was pleased to see that our table was still vacant – when had it become "our" table I wondered to myself. The bad weather seemed to have put off many of the tourists and other locals from venturing out.

We carried our drinks to the table and made ourselves comfortable. I was beginning to enjoy this routine, although I'd never really been much of a coffee-house patron before. Other than making "proper" coffee for breakfast for my Dad, I'd always made do with instant before. Was it the coffee or the company that was changing my tastes I wondered?

I suddenly realised Ben was watching me and I smiled, embarrassed. Had I tuned out and missed a question? He looked back at me with obvious concern etched across his handsome face. Before I could stop him, or divert his attention away, he gently reached over the table and lifted the sleeve of my shirt to reveal the bandage. My face must have been claret. I looked down at the table, refusing to meet his eyes as he waited for my reaction.

"Leah, what happened?" he asked the concern evident both in his voice and on his face.

"Oh it was nothing, just me being a clumsy idiot as usual. I slipped on the stairs and caught it on the banister," I lied, desperate to change the subject. The lie had come so easily, without having to think about it and that made me feel even worse. I hated having to lie and usually couldn't hide the fact that it was a lie.

"Leah, you can tell me anything, please understand that. If there is anything I can do to help, just say," he replied, resting his hand gently on my arm.

When I didn't reply he hesitated and then removed his hand slowly.

"I'm not going to pry Leah, if you tell me it was an accident then fine, I'll believe that that is what you want me to think. But I'm here if you need me and I want to be able to help you, if you want me to, that is."

I avoided his eyes again, "Thanks," I mumbled, mortified. "Honestly I am fine. What time are we meeting the others?" I asked, anxious to change the subject quickly.

Ben paused, obviously about to say something else but then decided to leave it and checked his watch instead.

"In about 20 minutes, so we've just got time to finish this coffee," he replied. I smiled at him gratefully and for a split second our eyes locked. It felt as though we were in a world of our own. I could have stayed like that forever.

Ben looked away first and blushing again, I reached forward for my cup, wincing at the movement. We finished our drinks in a slightly uncomfortable silence, I was hastily trying to think of a safe subject to turn the conversation to but my lie had frozen my mind. As I stared out of the window I frowned, the weather had turned really nasty again and the wind whipped along the little shopping area, picking up leaves and litter in its path. Just seeing it made me shudder, it was going to be much colder than I had thought. Ben must have followed my gaze, or saw my movement, because the next thing I knew he had carefully placed his jacket around my shoulders and when I started to object he gently placed his hand on my shoulder and shook his head. My shoulder smouldered at his touch.

I needed to stop this right now, how could this be right? How could I feel like this about a guy I hardly knew? I felt so safe and secure around him and yet I had known him barely a few weeks. I shook myself mentally. 'Watch yourself and don't lead him on, just because you're feeling vulnerable right now,' I thought to myself.

Surely it was not possible to fall for someone so quickly and I really wanted to stay friends with

Ben. For some reason it felt right to have him as part of my life and I didn't want to do anything stupid to make him hate me. I kept my eyes away from him, trying to work out how to get the balance right. My heart felt heavy just with the thought of it and I recognised in that instant that I really wanted more than just his friendship.

As I processed that perception, I realised that his hand was still on my shoulder. I looked up at him, wondering how I could move away without offending him – but I also had to accept the fact that I didn't actually want to move away. I shook myself again. Get a grip, I thought and made a move to stand up.

We looked towards the door at the same time. "I think we'd best run for it," I said, shuddering. I started to take his jacket off to return it.

"Don't be daft, you need it more than I do," he said and I thought I detected a hint of frustration in his voice. "Please don't be cross with me Leah, I can't help the way I am and I happen to believe that some things are right, even if you don't like it."

He took my elbow gently and steered me towards the door. Without any conscious communication, we seemed to take a deep breath at the same time and as Ben threw the door open, we ran together towards the car park. Before long, he was a good few strides ahead of me and I focussed everything on trying to catch up.

I never saw the bike coming as I ran down the street towards the car park. I heard the roar of a two stroke engine very close by and as I started to turn my head, I found myself flying through the air. I heard a scream, which I think came from me and the next thing I knew, I had landed hard and was skidding across the wet floor, heading straight for the walls of a shop forecourt. I put my hands out, desperately trying to stop myself, or at least slow myself down but it had no effect. I heard Ben shout and then it all went black as my body crashed into the wall.

Madness

When I came to there were strangers milling around. I could hear Ben's voice, low and urgent, talking to someone and I tried to work out where he was in the crowd around me. As my eyes began to focus, I saw him standing slightly to my side, talking urgently to what appeared to be another member of his band – I think it was Will. Cautiously, I struggled to look around, unsure of how badly I was injured, I didn't recognise anyone else. The motorbike was lying on its side not far from me and there was a small crowd gathered around a leather clad body lying motionless on the other side of the road, which I guessed must be the rider. I tried to raise my head in order to sit up, whimpering in the process and Ben was next to me in a flash.

"Don't try to move Leah, the ambulance is on its way, you got hit pretty bad." His voice was rough with worry and he crouched down by my side, gently resting his hand on my arm.

"What… what happened?" I asked trying desperately to recall. My mind was strikingly clear, although recollection of the event itself was far more difficult, I struggled to get up but Ben held me still, shaking his head.

"That … idiot … was going much too fast in this lousy weather. He hit the water and skidded into you. You're lucky to be alive," he replied. He glared over at the prone figure. "It's a good job that he is unconscious! Otherwise I might say, or even do, something that I would later regret, even in front of all these people."

I tried again to swing my legs around in order to sit up and winced. Everything hurt. Ben put a little pressure on my side as though encouraging, or even forcing me to stay still. Seconds later the ambulance sped to a stop, quickly followed by the police.

Ben walked straight over to the policeman. Watching him, or at least as well as I could from my semi-prone position, I was amazed at how calm he appeared, as he gave his account of what had happened. One of the paramedics came over and started to examine me.

"How are you doing sweetheart? You just lie there still for me for a second and let me take a look. No, you mustn't try to move, just let me examine you. What's your name, how old are you?" He rattled off questions and patter, whilst looking me over and assessing my injuries.

After he had completed the assessment, he swiftly wrapped a neck collar around me, while at the same time shouting for his partner to bring "the board". I tried to disagree but he shook his head.

"To be honest love you're lucky to be conscious at all. Looking at the damage you've done to this wall, I can't take the risk that you haven't got more serious injuries internally and the impact must have at least broken a few bones. It could just be the adrenaline that's enabling you to move and making you so calm. Just you lie there still and quiet for me, we will need to contact your next of kin. I'll go and get your boyfriend to come and sit with you. I'm sure he can give me the name and number, so just lie there and **keep still** until we can get you onto the bus and off to where they can check you over properly. I'm

just going to give you a little something for the pain."
Pretty soon I was strapped so tightly that I would
have barely been able to move, even if I had tried.
My head was totally immobile; as I registered this
knowledge, I felt a sharp scratch as he injected
something into my arm.

"He's not my….." I started to correct him but
then thought better of it. Ben came striding over,
with what I am sure he thought was a reassuring
smile on his face but I already knew him well enough
to know better.

"Ben, could you ring my Dad please?" I asked,
instinctively struggling to move, even though I knew
it would be impossible. As I spoke the paramedic ran
across to where his colleague was standing. "Where's
my bag? My phone is in it." For a split second I
thought I saw Ben's face change and then he shook
his head as he replied.

"Your bag is pretty messed up from the
accident, I think your phone will be beyond help.

Where does your Dad work – do you know the number?"

I tried to shake my head but the strapping prevented any movement at all. I hadn't bothered memorising the new number as I was so used to having my mobile. Fear started to surge through me. After last night, I dreaded to think what would happen, he would definitely be even angrier at what had happened today as well as being called out of work. I guess it was the thought of his anger, combined with the shock of the accident, because before I stood a chance of stopping them, I felt hot tears running down my cheeks.

"Hey, come on, don't fret, I'll find him for you." Ben urged, misunderstanding the primary cause of my tears. Fishing his own phone out of his pocket, he started dialling. Once again, I was amazed at how calm he appeared and before I knew it, he had tracked down which government agencies were based near the University. He dialled the number. "What's his name?" he asked me as he waited for an answer.

"Robert, Robert Clinton," I replied softly. For an instant his eyes widened at the name but before I could say any more he was speaking to someone at the other end.

"Hello? Yes, I need to speak to Robert Clinton please ….it is urgent….. I'm sure he would want to be disturbed. Please tell him that it is an urgent call and that it concerns his daughter."

I watched in astonishment as he responded to any argument the person at the other end had, pretty soon it was obvious he was talking to Dad.

"Hello? Mr Clinton? My name is Ben Edwards; I'm a friend of Leah's. Now, please don't be alarmed but there has been an accident. Leah was hit by a biker that lost control in the heavy rain. No, Mr Clinton, please don't worry, she is conscious and talking, although we don't know quite the extent of her injuries just yet. I am right here with her and I will go with her in the ambulance to the hospital. I promise that she won't be left on her own….. No, as I say, we don't know the extent of her injuries at the moment, there's no evidence of significant blood loss but they are concerned about internal injuries, it was a pretty hard knock. No, it's probably best that you meet us there Mr Clinton, they'll be moving her soon. Please, don't worry, I won't leave her, I promise, this is my number. If you could let me have your mobile number please, I will contact you again as soon as I know where she is and of course if anything changes."

I stared at him throughout the conversation, shocked at how calm and together he sounded, as though this was an everyday occurrence. As he hung up, he looked over at me and smiled reassuringly.

"Don't worry, he's leaving now and will meet us at the hospital," he said, crouching back down to me.

"How did you know where they were taking me?" I asked, struggling again to move, or at least turn my head and then wincing at the impact of the slightest futile movement.

"The paramedic told me when I said that I would make the call to your next of kin," he responded, frowning slightly as he witnessed my discomfort.

I tried to smile back at him. Why on earth was I being so awful to him? It wasn't as though he had done anything wrong- other than being a complete gentleman and looking after me, so why was I being so unreasonable?

I guess I just wasn't used to people being nice for the sake of it. I was always looking for their angle, judging them by the tabloid attitudes I saw daily in the newspaper.

Despite my erratic and ungrateful behaviour, Ben stayed by my side until the paramedics were ready to take me to hospital. Once he had confirmed that contact would swiftly be made with my next of kin, my paramedic had gone to help the others with the rider but judging by their reaction, it didn't look good. I shuddered as I thought about what could have been. I felt Ben's reassuring hand again and I smiled as I looked up, trying to convey my appreciation.

"You must be frozen!" I said, as I finally noticed his appearance. "Here, have your jacket back, I've got the blanket." I started struggling to move once more, a vain attempt to take my arm out of the sleeves, yet again the strapping did its' work. As I did so, I also chastised myself, how could I have been so selfish? Ben was absolutely soaked to the skin, his shirt clinging to his body from the rain. All this time he had been looking after me, in this awful weather, without a thought for his own wellbeing, no wonder his hand felt so cold on my shoulder.

"Shush, stop its ok. I'll be fine, I'm not the one that has been hurt," he murmured, trying to calm me. "Please, Leah, keep still, we still don't know just how badly you've been hurt and I don't want you risking any more damage to yourself. Now don't argue, please, just let me help you," he insisted.

How could I resist? The medication that the paramedic had given me must have finally started to work, because I starting getting the strangest, almost floating feeling, as though I wasn't really there. I watched Ben as closely as I could from my prone position, how he conducted himself with other people, the way he attended to me. Despite my current situation, I found myself secretly assessing and also being attracted by everything about him, the way he looked, even soaked to the skin, his voice, his behaviour.

I don't think I said anything to embarrass myself, or at least I hoped I didn't but I suddenly became conscious of a sound coming out of my mouth. It wasn't a word, or even a moan; it was an expression of pain- "hnnnnhh". I tried to move again, becoming abruptly aware of the awkward way in which I was strapped onto this board. I also was soaked completely through to the skin. As he became aware of my movement and what it meant, Ben glanced very quickly at my face, extracted himself from where he'd been crouching next to me, sheltering slightly from the rain and ran over to the other side of the road to alert the paramedics.

They looked back at me and although I couldn't hear what was said, I could tell by the earnest manner with which they spoke that something was going to happen. Without any further warning, the driver of one of the ambulances was at my side and my paramedic was running back to me across the road, which the police were trying to reopen. Without saying a word they scooped me up on the board and rushed me to the ambulance.

"nnnhhn, b,b,b,nnnh" I slurred, trying desperately to get Ben's attention, as he started to move away.

"It's alright Leah, I'm coming right with you, I just need a second." He motioned to the paramedic that he would be right back and I saw him go off to the left and start talking quickly to someone. I quickly recognised Will from the band and saw Ben hand over his keys. Will nodded and Ben turned and ran back to the ambulance. Jumping in, the paramedic slammed the door behind him and shouted to the driver to go.

To my embarrassment, we proceeded to fly through the streets, sirens and lights flashing. I was still trying to talk to someone but no intelligible sound would come out of my mouth. I looked up at the ceiling and hot tears of frustration started to slide down my cheeks. Ben tried to come to my side but was immediately pushed back in his seat by the paramedic.

"It's alright, I'm here and we'll soon get you sorted. If I can't go to her, can't you at least do something; you can see how upset she is." He demanded of the paramedic, his frustration evident in his voice.

The paramedic grabbed something from the shelf above and gently dried my face. I felt even more ashamed and started trying to explain.

"Don't try to talk, the effect of the drugs means that your words are slurring. We'll soon be at the hospital and your father will probably already be there." Was that a hint of anger I heard in Ben's voice?

I lay there staring up at the ceiling of the ambulance, hearing the sirens wail as we wound our way to the hospital. What was I doing? Ben had been so good to me and yet all I could do was doubt him. Suddenly it dawned on me that I had already developed very real feelings for him. Was **that** the problem, was I still so scared of admitting that I could care for someone, in fact, that I needed someone in my life?

After Mom, I had built a wall around myself, not allowing anyone to get close. It hadn't been that difficult, I'd always kept myself apart from the other kids back home, so they didn't really notice the change and it was easy for me to dissuade any boy who had shown an interest –they'd hardly even noticed the push back. Dad… well, he hardly noticed either. We hadn't exactly been close before and although he sometimes tried, he really didn't have a clue about how to get through to me and quickly lost his temper as a result. My best friend, Jen, had been the only other person in my life that I had ever let get that close.

Ben was different though. Despite my best attempts to push him away, he had got closer and somehow found a crack in the wall, which he had managed to squeeze through. I had to admit to myself that it felt right; it was good to have someone that close to me. I finally admitted to myself what the problem was. I wanted him to be even closer. It was that thought, the entire concept of letting someone get close enough to hurt me that badly, **that** was the real problem.

As I finally accepted that truth, I tried to turn my head to look at him. The head brace, made this impossible but Ben, attentive as ever, noticed the movement and tried to reposition himself into my line of sight. The paramedic glared at him as he moved.

"I'm sorry," I whispered, trying to hide the huge effort it took to speak coherently and convey everything I wanted to say with those two simple words.

"There's nothing to be sorry for, just focus on getting better, please," he insisted and the warmth in his voice made my heart race. I listened nervously to the monitors, would the paramedic be able to tell what I was feeling? I lay there for a while, listening to the sirens and thinking through the realisation and everything that it could mean.

My thoughts were interrupted with Ben, who spoke gently. I could still just about see his face from where I was lying and I could see that he was smiling tenderly.

"It's alright Leah, don't worry, we've got as long as we need, we can talk later. I promise I am not going anywhere," he said. At that point, the ambulance came to an abrupt stop and the paramedic threw the doors open.

Organised chaos seemed to follow, the bright lights of the hospital corridors, lots of different faces in uniform and strange voices. But throughout it all, the constant at the centre of this chaos was Ben, always by my side, always reassuring me with a touch, or a smile, talking earnestly to the medical staff, explaining everything a hundred times. Where **did** he get his patience from I wondered.

Suddenly I heard a familiar voice.

"Where is she? I demand to see my daughter!" My father's voice was gruff but was there fear there as well as anger? I hoped so but the hope was brief as he barged into the room. Ben went to try to introduce himself, only to be pushed out of the way.

"Leah, I'm here, everything is going to be just fine. I'll get you home as soon as I can," he said. Where was the concern, the tenderness, the asking questions? I could easily understand the panic but what was this anger all about?

Ben tried again. "Hello Mr Clinton, I'm Ben Edwards, I was with Leah when the accident happened." Before he could even finish his sentence my father rounded on him:

"So, it's your fault is it? What are you doing sniffing around my daughter in the first place? She's much too young for you and to get her involved in bikes, well, really! Get out of this room and **never** come near my daughter again or you will have me to answer to and believe me, **I** can make your life not worth living!"

I heard myself gasp, both at his words and the pure venom in his voice.

"Ben!" I heard myself gasp. "Don't go, please, you promised…."

Dad rounded on me then, "Shut up Leah, you need to keep yourself quiet. It is this idiot's fault you're in here and I want him out of your life, for good!" he ranted. I could tell that whatever had riled him the night before still hadn't gone away.

I shook my head, dazed both from the medication and from his words and attitude. I tried taking some deep breaths, to steady my voice before I spoke.

At my father's outburst, Ben flushed, then he turned away, as though he was about to leave the room. But as I began speaking, he stopped, hand still on the door handle and turned his head back toward the room, as if to listen to what I was starting to say.

"Dad," I started, pleased at the strength in my voice. "Ben is my friend. If it wasn't for him, I would probably be in a much worse state and the accident was not his fault. I want him to stay."

As I finished, I saw a brief smile cross Ben's face and he turned towards my father, speaking before Dad got the chance to argue.

"Mr Clinton, I am sorry you feel that way but I can assure you that it was never my intention for Leah to get hurt. As for the bike, well, neither of us had anything to do with that. We were on the way to my car and for that I will take responsibility. The bike, however, lost control in this awful storm and hit Leah as we were running on the pavement and with all due respect, Sir, I fail to see how that could be **either** of our faults." He paused, as he took a deep breath before continuing.

"However, as you have just heard Leah herself express her wish that I stay, I will remain here at the hospital and afterward, by her side, for as long as she wishes. Whether **you** permit it or not."

I stared at him in awe, it must have really taken some nerve to respond to my father in this way and again I was struck by how calm he appeared. The same could not however be said of my father, his face was purple with rage.

"**She** will do as I tell her, **I** am **her** father and **she** is still a child!" He bellowed.

I couldn't help myself but jump at the tone in his voice and the bruise on my arm, which had been hidden by Ben's jacket during the accident and was now bandaged like the rest of me, throbbed faintly in memory of the last time he had displayed such rage. I felt myself cower back into the bedclothes at his voice but the echo of Ben's words came back to me. I took another deep breath to steady my nerves, so that I could speak up again.

"Dad, I am nineteen years old. You cannot force me to tell Ben to leave if I don't want him to and you need to accept the fact that **I do not want him to leave**." I was surprised at the strength in my voice, because inside I was shaking like a leaf. I had never disobeyed either of my parents like this before.

He rounded on me with a noise that sounded suspiciously like a snarl and for a second I thought he was going to hurt me again, like he had the night before. Although I was looking straight at Dad, out of the corner of my eye I caught a movement and to my surprise, Ben was suddenly standing by my side, right next to my father.

"Mr Clinton, I can see how upset you are and that is completely understandable. But, please understand that I would **never** allow **anything,** or **anyone,** to harm Leah. The doctors are doing their rounds right now, so why don't you go and get yourself a drink and try to calm down a little, Leah is in good hands now." His words were said calmly and with respect but there was an underlying edge to them.

That strange noise came from my father again but he seemed to listen, because with a quick glance back at me, he stormed out of the room, shutting the door loudly behind him. My nerve finally broke and I started to shake from head to toe.

Ben was instantly aware of the change. He perched on the side of the bed, careful not to touch me in case it hurt but as close as he could get otherwise. He looked at me for a moment and then shook his head sadly. "Why didn't you tell me Leah?" He asked quietly.

"Tell you what?" I asked, hedging, although why, I wasn't sure. The whole thing was now blatantly obvious.

"What it is like at home? I now realise how you "hurt" your arm, I saw the finger marks when they redressed it but I never dreamt it was **him**." He noticed my alarm and added, "It's ok; I don't think anyone else noticed. They were too busy recording the rest of your injuries. You don't need to put up with it Leah, no-one can treat you like **this.**" The pain was evident in his voice and etched onto his face. It took the last remnants of my strength not to give in to the threatening tears and beg him to get me away from here, to make it all go away.

"It hasn't always been like this," I replied, desperate to make him understand. "Yesterday was the first time, honestly. I've never seen him like this before. Yes, he has a bad temper and often shouts and screams if I do something wrong but he has never raised his hand to me before yesterday." However even as I said it, a vague memory crept unbidden into my mind.

"What is it Leah, are you in pain?" Ever attentive, Ben had noticed the change. I shook my head, trying to dispel the unwanted images in my mind.

Suddenly I was afraid, really afraid. I tried closing my eyes but the images behind my lids were even worse, so instead I looked at Ben, seeking comfort.

"Tell me, please, you **can** trust me Leah, you don't have to deal with this on your own anymore." He was almost whispering.

That phrase and the way it was said, echoed with a memory but I couldn't bring it into focus at the moment.

"I've never known Dad to be like this with me," I began, "honestly," I added hastily when I saw the sceptical look in his eyes.

"He has never treated me badly, especially since Mom….." I trailed off again, even here now, with Ben, I couldn't bring myself to voice the words.

"But I remember, for about six months before that, he and Mom would have these massive arguments, I'd forgotten, I suppose, buried them, until now. I never knew what they were about, I don't even think Mom knew – we were so close there were times when I could have sworn I could hear what she was thinking but Dad would suddenly fly off the handle, just like now. He would scream and shout at her for hours at a time." I hesitated and Ben gently squeezed my hand that was lying next to him on the bed.

"There was a time towards the end when I thought he might be hurting her, because there were a few occasions when she would have these terrible bruises. Once on her face, as though she had been slapped hard and other times on her arms or legs. She always dismissed them as being nothing though – she had walked into an open cupboard, fallen down some steps, she always had an excuse but now, now….." I couldn't bring myself to say it and I really didn't even want to think it was possible. "Ben, you don't think…" It came out as a sob and I turned my head away, not wanting him to see my fears.

"Shush, don't even think about that. He's probably just got a lot on his mind at the moment and just over-reacted. I'm sure he didn't mean to do anything," he soothed.

Through my fear crept his strange choice of words. I shuddered.

I didn't have time to think any further about it though, as the door opened and in walked a doctor. He didn't look that much older than Ben and I.

"Good afternoon Miss Clinton, my name is Dr Woods and I am your doctor," he said, in a quiet, authoritative tone, which immediately made him appear older than he looked.

Ben threw a concerned look at me and I could tell that he thought I was just too fragile to deal with anything else right now.

"Hello Doctor," he replied, leaving the edge of the bed and moving to the chair. He grabbed the front of it and pulled it forward, so it was still as close to me as he could get. I jumped at the scraping sound that it made.

"Well, Miss Clinton, you are a very lucky young lady. By rights, you should be in a much worse condition than you are – despite the force of your impact, which, from what I hear, almost completely demolished the wall, you only appear to have a few broken ribs, the humerus of your right arm and the leg of course. However it still a little early to be completely certain that there aren't any further injuries. We would, therefore, like to keep you in here for just a few days, as I am still concerned about concussion and there are signs that there may be some internal bleeding.

You hit your head with some considerable force and the extent of your wounds and bruising are quite significant. They are likely to cause you some considerable discomfort over the next few days. Nothing serious to worry about right now but still, I would prefer to keep an eye on you for a few days?" He ended the sentence as though it was a question and I realised that he was asking me, telling me that they couldn't actually keep me here if I wanted to leave. Ben reached forward and put his hand on my left arm and squeezed gently. I looked at him but couldn't quite decipher what his eyes were trying to tell me.

I nodded at the doctor, who smiled and started writing on my chart and I felt Ben's hand relax. As Dr Woods put the chart back on the end of my bed, the door to my room opened and in walked my father again. I felt my body tense as the atmosphere in the room veered from the restful calm to fully charged. Ben's hand tightened again, he was trying to reassure me. I saw my father take in the quick movement and his eyes narrowed.

"Well, **Doctor**," he almost sneered the words, "When can I take her home?" Even as he spoke, he was already throwing open the closet and cupboards looking for my things.

"Not just yet Mr... erm... Clinton?" The doctor looked down at my notes to determine the surname and I noticed that he suddenly seemed to have more authority in his voice than before. "I'm afraid we are keeping Leah here for a few days, both to keep an eye on her known injuries and also to rule out any internal injuries and concussion. I need to remind you that normal hospital visiting hours are between two and four and then seven and nine each afternoon and evening and no more than two visitors are allowed at any one time. The doctor's rounds will be at ten every morning, where we will review Leah's progress and discuss things with her. As she is now legally an adult, I must point out that we can only discuss her condition and progress with her, unless we have her express permission to do otherwise." He glanced at me and nodded slightly as he said that and it took all my strength to stifle the sound as the realisation dawned that he had heard every word that had been said earlier. Of that I was certain and I was utterly mortified.

Dad turned and glared at me but I avoided looking at him. I needed to get my thoughts straight before I could face him properly and although I despised hospitals, at least this gave me some breathing space. If I was honest, it also provided the safety that I was suddenly longing for.

"Okay," I said clearly, before Dad could speak, indicating my acceptance of staying at the hospital. I didn't need to look to know that the hiss that I heard had come from my Father.

The Doctor nodded at me and left the room without any further comment. Ben stood up and I turned my head to look at him. He smiled gently and moved his head so slightly I doubted if anyone else would have caught the change.

"Leah, I'm going to go check in with Will and Richard, find out what they've done with my car and whether Lady Bess is still in one piece. I won't leave the hospital and I **will** be back in 10 minutes," he said, his eyes never leaving mine. I gave him a small nervous smile. I was suddenly frightened to be left alone with my own Father. He smiled at me reassuringly and without speaking to Dad he left the room.

Reluctantly I turned my head towards Dad, afraid of what I would see on his face, or of what he was going to say.

To my surprise, he greeted me with a sheepish expression on his face.

"I'm sorry Leah, I really don't know what got into me, I guess I was just really worried and I let it get the better of me, I really am sorry," he said, smiling now.

Somehow though, I didn't believe a word he said. For a split second of acute and painful insight, I saw that he was trying to placate me, fool me into leaving the hospital and going home with him. Deep inside I knew that as soon as I was away from this relative safety, his temper would return and I would be in just as much danger as before, if not more. I just couldn't work out why, surely it couldn't be just because of Ben and I'd barely known him long enough to break my promise.

I smiled back, although if he had paid any real and genuine attention he would have known it was a false smile. My heart sank as the realisation dawned that I would never feel the same way again about the man that was my father. That hero-worship that all little girls have for their Daddy had well and truly been destroyed. At this point in time, I didn't think I could even bring myself back to trusting him again.

I swallowed hard. I had always loved my Dad; I think most little girls do. Even though we weren't kindred spirits, not like Mom and I, it had always been a silence filled with love and understanding. Conversations about certain things were difficult but I always knew that he cared and that he was there for me, just as I was for him. Now that had been destroyed, perhaps forever, by a few moments of uncontrollable anger.

I turned my head towards the window. Misreading my silence for acceptance, Dad started to talk. More words than I could remember us ever sharing before in one single conversation came pouring out, as though he was saying anything to fill the silence that lay like a void between us. He talked about what the doctor had said, what he'd been up to at work when the call came, how he had supposedly felt and anything else he could think of. There were just two subjects that he avoided, the first being Ben – even going as far as to refer to "that boy" rather than have to mention his name; and the second being what had happened between us the day before.

After what felt like an age but could really only have been twenty minutes, he finally seemed to get the message.

"Anyway Sweetheart," he said. "I suppose I'd better let you get your rest now, before they throw me out and refuse to let me back in. Night Night, sleep well and I'll be here as soon as visiting hours start in the morning." I felt myself tense as he leant over me to kiss me goodbye but I resisted the urge to turn away. Finally, after what had felt like an eternity, he was gone.

I lay there watching the shadows change as the afternoon faded. Pretty soon the medication started taking effect and I found myself starting to drift off. As I floated off, I had the strangest feeling that I wasn't alone, I struggled to open my eyes to see but the weight of the drugs pulled me under.

"Leah, it's alright, I'm here with you as always, just as I promised," Mom's voice crept into my consciousness. I felt myself smile and finally started to relax. Now I knew that everything would be okay.

"You were hurt pretty bad sweetheart and I'm sorry I couldn't stop that but you just rest and allow yourself to get better. I love you Baby. Everything will be fine don't you worry. It will all make sense in

the end. The worst part is over, I promise but it will be a while yet until you fully understand.

Make sure you watch over her and keep her safe, won't you?"

It took me a moment or two to register that last comment. Look after who, who was she talking about but just as it sank in and I started to think about it, I heard a second, also somehow familiar, voice,

*"Don't worry, I will. Nothing else is going to hurt her. You need to go now, it is much too soon for her to understand everything but I promise I **will** keep her safe."*

Even as I tried to work out who the second voice was, I sank deeper into the drug induced oblivion.

Alone

I finally awoke several hours later. For a brief moment I was confused, dazed and then the events of the last few days came crashing back.

Unfortunately, the pain came with it but this was like a steamroller flattening me and squashing any thought of trying to move. I sank back into the bed with a muffled groan.

In a flash someone was by my side; hand on my arm, looking down. Before I even opened my eyes, I knew it was Ben and despite myself, I felt safe once more.

I slowly opened my eyes and looked up at him. I could see my reflection mirrored in his eyes and for a brief second I wondered how anyone could ever find **this** attractive. I pushed that thought out of my mind. I was too pleased to see him, to have him here with me to let those thoughts intrude and spoil it.

I tried to smile but from the reflection it looked more of a grimace. He nodded and smiled gently, then leaving me he went to the door to stop a nurse that was passing, to ask for my medication.

Within a few minutes Dr Woods was back in the room, checking the recent notes on my chart and injecting something into the drip.

"Leah, your father called to tell you not to worry. Apparently you missed your tablet this morning? He said to tell you it won't hurt for one day and he will bring them with him when he visits tomorrow.

Can I ask what medication it is that you are taking?"

For a brief moment I was completely mystified, then it dawned on me and I grinned.

"I'm not, I've taken a special vitamin supplement for about five years now, Dad gets them from some herbalist but it is only vitamins. It hadn't even dawned on me that I'd forgotten to take it, in fact I don't think I've taken it for a few days. I can't believe Dad was that worried, it's not as if it's life threatening"

Dr Woods nodded, glanced over at Ben and then left without saying another word.

Ben waited until the door had closed.

"Leah, I'd like make a suggestion if that is ok with you?" he began and I glanced at him, startled by the degree of formality in his tone. I raised my eyebrows to him and taking that as acknowledgement he continued.

"Whilst you were asleep, I rang my Father – really just to let him know everything was ok and he came to the hospital to see me. I don't know if you heard him when he came in? We went downstairs and grabbed a coffee in the end as I didn't want to disturb you. Don't be concerned, I didn't tell him much about your situation; we just talked about the accident. Anyway, to cut a long story short, Dr Woods came in whilst we were talking. He and my father have met before and they started chatting. My Father suggested we have you moved to The Chase, at our expense, so that you can have dedicated one to one care. Dr Woods apparently holds consultations there, so he would be able to continue to be responsible for your care. Would that be okay with you?" I heard the hesitation in his voice as he trailed off.

I smiled over at him, taking a deep breath while I quickly thought through what I wanted to say, while also desperately trying to convince myself that it was an action of friendship and concern, nothing else.

"What is there to mind, Ben? I know you are only worried and are trying to do what's best for me. It might make things worse with my Dad though, if he sees you doing something for me that he can't."

As I talked, it occurred to me that Ben never referred to his own father as Dad. It was always in the much more formal "My Father", which felt very strange. My muddled thoughts were interrupted as Ben continued,

"I don't think your Dad would have a problem Leah, after all, they will be providing excellent care for you and the visiting hours are far more flexible. He doesn't need to know the full story, or that I will be staying there too, as that might make things worse."

I looked at him in surprise, suddenly very worried that something was wrong. Had Ben also been injured during the accident and not told me? There had been no sign of any injury at the time. Noting the change in my expression he shook his head quickly.

"No, I'm fine, honestly. I'll be staying there so that I can look after you and be with you, just like I promised. When your Dad visits I'll go to my room until he has gone but I will be right there for you if the need arises."

My heart sank at his words. Is that really what my life had come to? Did I need a twenty four hour bodyguard in case my father turned violent? I shuddered at the thought but still, in my memory echoed the arguments that I had overheard between him and Mom.

How I wished she were here to talk to right now.

Ben must have sensed my darkening mood, because he was back by my side in an instant. He placed his hand on my shoulder gently, to reassure me.

"You are the one in control here Leah, I won't make you do anything you don't want to. Just tell me what you want and I will make it happen for you."

I smiled up at him, considering his words. For a few seconds, the medication must have taken over, because I allowed my mind to dwell on how wonderful it would be if Ben really could make that happen. What would I ask to happen?

To have my Mom to talk to and comfort me?

For Dad to be **my** Dad, the one of my childhood memories and not this hideous, violent replica?

To be able to fall asleep and not have those terrifying dreams?

Reluctantly I dragged my mind back to a more realistic present. None of the above would be possible and I knew it would be both ridiculous and also unfair of me to ask.

I thought about his offer for a moment. I had to admit the concept of a quiet room to myself, my own private bathroom, a television to while away some of the boredom and, if I was honest, Ben's company, were all extremely inviting at the moment.

Ben was watching me closely as my mind processed the fantasy and realistic thought processes. In the end I sighed sadly:

"That would be extremely generous of your father, Ben." Now I was using the more formal phrase. "But how could I ever repay your generosity?" I continued quickly as he went to protest. "Even if I agreed to your offer, which I admit is very tempting, we would also need to ensure that Dad was comfortable with everything before we went ahead."

He nodded and turned his head away for an instant. For a brief moment I panicked – had I said something that had somehow offended him, or upset him in some other way.

I quickly ran through my words again in my head, trying to work out what I had said or done wrong. As I was considering this and wondering how to repair the damage he turned back to look at me.

Seeing the look on my face, he smiled that warm, gentle smile at me again and without warning, my stomach started to churn once more.

"Don't worry Leah, you haven't said anything to upset me, I was just trying to think through the best way to approach it with your Dad." I swallowed hard. How was it that he could understand my deepest fears without my ever having voiced them?

Perhaps Ben was starting to feel something for me too? I pushed that thought away as quickly as it had come. I couldn't afford to let such impossible thoughts raise my hopes in this way. Ben was simply being a gentleman. He obviously felt guilty about the accident, not that it was by any means his fault and was simply trying to look after me. That was all it was, all it could be. There was no way in this world that someone like Ben could fall for a nonentity like me.

Ben spoke again, interrupting my thoughts.

"I think the best thing would be for Dr Woods to speak to your father, before morning if possible. He can explain what we have offered and suggest that in his medical opinion it would be the best option for you. In terms of the care and recovery you need, appealing to his paternal feelings toward you. Your Dad can't really argue with that and as he has made it clear he blames me for the whole thing, he will probably see it as some form of recompense for what you've been put through." He nodded slowly, with a slight scowl on his face as though satisfied with this solution even though he disagreed with the thoughts behind it.

I had to admit, it made sense and he was right, if Dad heard it from the Doctor, rather than either Ben or myself, he was more likely to accept it, or at least, less likely to argue.

"Ok" I said and Ben smiled.

"Right then, I'll go and have a quick chat with Dr Woods and explain our plan. Hopefully he will be able to contact your father quickly and then we can get you transferred first thing in the morning."

He glanced quickly at his watch. "On that note, I really must be going before someone calls security on me," he laughed as he said it and for the first time

I looked over toward the clock on the wall – it was over half an hour past the official end of visiting hours.

My heart sank. I really didn't want to be left here alone all night. I could feel the medication starting to work again as I was beginning to get drowsy but the last thing I needed was to have one of **those** dreams again, right here in the hospital. That would be completely impossible to explain.

Ben gently squeezed my arm again, said his goodbyes and left quietly, glancing quickly over his shoulder at me as he left. Was he as sorry to leave, I wondered, as I was to see him go? Stop that now, you stupid girl I thought to myself with a grimace. He is well and truly out of your league.

I scolded myself for allowing this pipe dream to continue. To take my mind off it I took the opportunity to look around this temporary home. It was a small hospital bay, only large enough for two beds but the second was empty at the moment. The bay had walls on three sides and each bed had a curtain that would go around it, to provide privacy.

That was debatable of course, because a curtain hardly provided soundproofing. It was no wonder Dr Woods had reacted to my father the way he had, he would have heard every single word that had been said.

I shuddered again, it was best not to think about that at the moment, it would only get me more upset and bring on the nightmares. Instead I found myself drifting off into heavy, drug-induced sleep thinking about Mom and the fun we'd had together. There she was again, her sweet voice telling me she was here with me and always would be. The calmness engulfed me, as it had when I was a child ill in bed whenever she was with me.

I tried to roll over in my sleep, as I would have done had I been in my own bed and the discomfort of the injuries and the hospital bed, woke me up. I lay there for a second, as the sensation that I was not alone crept slowly into my consciousness. I tried not to react – after all it was probably just a nurse.

"It's ok Leah sweetheart, I'm here with you and always will be, just as I promised" Mom said.

I jumped and turned my head much too quickly. Pain shot through my shoulders and neck. Of course there was no-one there, that was really not going to happen but her voice had been so clear. I must have still been dreaming and the medication was causing me to hallucinate, that was the only logical conclusion.

I lay there staring at the ceiling for what felt like hours, desperately trying to get back to sleep but unable to get comfortable on the bed due to my injuries and the pain. The clock on the wall said 3am, so it would be hours before I would get any company. I wondered where Ben was, what he was doing and whether he was ok. Probably fast asleep like you should be, I reprimanded myself. But just the thought of him gave me comfort and alone there in my hospital bed, I finally had to admit to myself that I had fallen for him, hard.

How **could** I allow myself to fall for someone I knew so little about? I'd always been so cautious around boys, never letting them get close enough to know me and therefore protecting myself from getting hurt. Somehow, Ben had crept up and got through my armour unnoticed, leaving me completely unprepared for these feelings but despite the unknown, it still felt right.

Quietly, I laughed at my thoughts. I was making it sound as though he had manipulated the situation and deliberately got me to fall in love with him. All he had really done was to be friendly, take me for who I actually am and tried to look after me. What could be wrong with that?

As I thought about him, his face floated before me in my mind, with that gorgeous, gentle smile and eyes that I could drown in forever. There was no going back now, wherever this connection between us had come from, it was now a permanent link. Like it or not, I had fallen in love with this man, the term "boy" really did not seem to fit Ben at all, and nothing was going to change that fact. I couldn't hold him responsible, they were my emotions after all and if I got hurt as a result, I had only myself to blame.

My thoughts turned to their offer. It was extremely generous, private hospital beds did not come cheap. Neither did the nursing time and Dr Woods' fees, I was sure of that. Every inch of me ached to be able to read more into their kindness but I kept reminding myself that they were doing it out of some kind of misguided obligation. Why they should feel duty bound though, I couldn't say.

My head was really throbbing now, even thinking hurt. I looked at the clock again, it was no use, I was going to have to ring and ask for more pain relief. I gently felt around with my hands and finally found the call button.

Within seconds Dr Woods was by my side.

"Don't you ever sleep?" I asked surprised to see him still here.

"I'm on duty this evening and you are **my** patient. How are you feeling?" he asked, checking the monitors which were still attached.

"As though I've been hit by a truck... or should that be a bike?" I joked, trying to mask how bad I actually was now feeling. "It's just any kind of movement really, although I have to say that my head is killing me," I added.

Dr Woods frowned and examined my eyes closely without saying anything. He then got another syringe from a drawer, checked the label and then injected it into the drip.

"That should help a little Leah, although that headache does worry me. Don't wait so long next time before asking for help – we can manage your pain better for you if we keep on top of it rather than wait until it is unbearable. In other words, don't be a martyr." He smiled and then left as quickly as he had arrived.

I turned my head gently to look out of the small window. The bad weather had obviously lifted for now and I could make out some of the stars, although the moon was out of sight. Whatever Doctor Woods had given me, it worked quickly, because I was soon drifting back off.

*"Leah, you must remember, **trust your instincts** and follow your heart, it will not let you down I promise. I love you my darling." Mom's voice swirled around me as I slipped back into a dreamless sleep.*

Security

I need not have worried. Whatever drugs Dr Woods had given to me easily kept the nightmares at bay that night, so at least I didn't humiliate myself in the hospital. By the time I awoke, the room was quite bright and the clock said 8:15am. I was surprised, as this was quite late for me as a rule.

Slowly, as I came back to my senses, I realised that there was quite a lot of activity going on in the little bay and I cautiously tried to turn my head so that I could see what was happening.

Ben had his back to me and was sorting through the clothes in the little cupboard. They were the ones that they had cut off me yesterday and he was obviously looking to see if anything was salvageable – I could have told him not to bother, they hadn't been careful with the scissors.

As I watched he got to his jacket. With relief I remembered that they had managed to remove that without the scissors – at least he wouldn't have lost that.

Then he lifted it up and I stifled a gasp. One shoulder was almost completely shredded – which must have happened as I slid across the pavement towards the wall. I cringed as I looked at the damage. It was a miracle I'd got away without anything worse than a couple of broken bones and severe bruising, at this stage I was ignoring Dr Woods' concerns about possible internal bleeding. As I gently tried to flex my muscles though, I had to admit that I really didn't feel that lucky.

I continued to watch quietly as Ben fished his phone from his pocket, selected a speed dial and held it to his ear. He spoke so quietly I could barely make out his words but I did catch, "nothing, size ten," and I realised he was talking to someone about my clothes and embarrassingly, what size I took.

As he hung up he glanced toward me and I wasn't quick enough to turn away. He smiled as he saw that I had been watching him.

"I'm afraid all of these things need to go in the bin," he began, gesturing towards the pile.

"I'm sorry about your jacket…" I began and he shook his head, interrupting me quickly.

"I can't think of a better use for it than protecting you, even if it was only just a little bit in yesterday's mayhem. Please don't worry, I can easily get another."

He didn't have time to say anything else, because the room suddenly became even busier. Dr Woods, did that man **ever** sleep, entered the room, along with two other men, both dressed in a green uniform, manipulating a trolley between them. The three of them were deep in conversation.

"Leah. I'm glad to see that you are awake now. These gentlemen are going to move you to The Chase, as we discussed yesterday. I'm going to give you some more pain relief and also a sedative, to make the journey bearable. The staff there will get you settled and comfortable. They already have details of your medication and will monitor you concerning your internal injuries. Unless I am called in earlier, I shall see you there tomorrow morning, after I've slept." He grinned quickly at me then as though he had heard my thoughts, then continued, "I spoke to your father last night and he was happy to agree to Mr Edwards' suggestion. He will see you there this afternoon, as there are one or two things he needs to deal with at work first."

As he was completing this conversation, he started to inject two syringes into the IV – within seconds I felt myself start to drift off.

"Ben…!" I suddenly panicked, I couldn't go on my own, I needed him there with me.

"It's alright Leah, I am coming with you. My father dropped me off this morning so that I could travel in the ambulance with you. I promise I will not leave you." As he said this he was back at my side, gently touching my arm and I let the medication continue to take effect as I relaxed in the comfort of his continued presence.

***

I have absolutely no idea what happened on the journey to The Chase. I know that journey would have taken about half an hour in terms of travel time but I was out cold for much longer than that. When I finally came round, I found myself fully installed into my own private suite. I was in a hospital bed, although the name was the closest resemblance it had to the one I had tried to sleep in the previous night. It seemed as though every single part of the bed could be raised, tilted, or adjusted in one way or another to ensure maximum comfort and even the rails could be lowered with the touch of a button. The "hospital" linen was best quality Egyptian cotton and everything about the room radiated quality. From my bed I could see the small flat screen TV and an area through the archway that was more of a "living" area, with a larger TV, comfortable chaise longue and two armchairs. I could also see at least two telephones, one in the bedroom area and the other next to the TV in the lounge. There was one door that I could see off the archway, which I assumed either led to the rest of the hospital, or perhaps the bathroom.

I tried to sit up and groaned. This was ridiculous, at the end of the day I was simply badly bruised. Surely I should be able to at least sit myself up! I succumbed to the pain and examined the bed remote control, using it to adjust my position so I wasn't lying down.

It must have been the sound of the motor, because within a few seconds, I heard the sound of a door opening and from the opposite side of the archway to the doorway that I could see, Ben walked in. He smiled in genuine relief when he saw me and came quickly to my side.

I resisted his attempts to take the controls and finished getting myself into what I felt was a more suitable position, although I was concerned to find that I was in nice, clean, expensive nightclothes. Ben saw my look and noting my sudden embarrassment, he couldn't hide his grin.

"Don't panic, it was all very proper, I was excused from the room whilst the nurses checked your dressings and got you changed, I didn't see anything." Seeing my puzzled look he added, "they arranged for the clothes to be delivered here from Leamington Spa, part of the service they offer to their *special* guests."

Although relieved that at least my modesty had been spared, I couldn't help wondering about the comment, why was I any more special than any of their other guests? I started to ask but my head hurt so much that I decided against it.

Attentive as ever, Ben noticed the change, reached across the bed and pressed the red call button on the bed control. It was the closest he had been to me since the accident and my realisation of what he had started to mean to me and having him this close to me set my whole body tingling. I was frightened to breathe in case I gave myself away. His eyes caught mine and for a split second I was lost again, drowning in their depths. The moment was lost though as a very professional looking, gorgeous, nurse entered the room. Despite the luxurious surroundings and expensive clothing, I suddenly felt extremely out of place. She flashed a perfect smile at Ben and then bustled around me, taking my blood pressure and temperature, recording them on my chart and without speaking to me, injecting another dose of something into the contraption in my hand.

It was only then that I realised that the drip, although I had been assured it was only saline anyway, had been removed while I was unconscious. All that was left was the needle in my hand, to which the drip had been attached, which the nurse removed and then replaced, some kind of cap from. She gave Ben another dazzling smile as she left, still without having said a word to me.

I raised my eyebrows at her back as she left. I didn't need to say anything. Ben knew exactly what I was querying

"Don't worry, it is common practice that they will not disturb you, or speak directly to you, unless you speak to them first – unless of course there is an emergency. Some of their more exclusive… erm… *guests*, prefer complete anonymity."

I nodded. Although that still seemed a bit extreme to me, I wasn't about to argue with him, he would know far better than I.

To be honest though, I didn't get much choice. A sudden commotion erupted from outside and my heart sank. I would know that voice anywhere. I glanced at Ben with sudden alarm; didn't he need to get out of here before my father came into the room? Ben just smiled at me and stayed exactly where he was. I closed my eyes. I really did not have the strength for another argument right now. To my total amazement though, he seemed to be having an argument with someone in the corridor, about, of all things, my vitamin tablets and needing to take them now. I shook my head in frustration – they were vitamins for goodness sake and I was in one of the best hospitals in the country, I was hardly going to suffer from malnutrition in here!

I heard the nurse close the conversation swiftly by telling him that medication was only administered at certain times of the day, when there was a doctor on site but she gave him her word that I would have them at the next round. She continued swiftly, advising him that she had been told of the "incident" at my bedside yesterday. She would not tolerate behaviour like that, as it was her priority to keep me calm and help me recover as quickly as possible. She finished the conversation by telling him that if a similar disturbance arose today, she would have him immediately escorted from the premises. The silence told me that Dad had accepted this, which surprised me but then I supposed he felt that he had no choice and **he** didn't know that I had only just been given medication.

Ben smiled at me and then stood. As he passed the bed, he gently squeezed my arm again and walking briskly, he met my father as he opened the door.

For a brief moment they just looked at one another, I saw Dad's eyes narrow at the sight of him but he didn't say a word, just pushed past him into the room. I saw him look around quickly, taking the room, its contents and the luxury in all at once. As he did so, Ben turned to face him, a calm expression on his face.

"Now that you are here, Mr Clinton, I'm going to get off home. I promised Leah that I wouldn't leave until you arrived, so she wasn't on her own here. She is still very sore, Mr Clinton and Dr Woods has advised that she remain calm, rest and stay in bed for today, until we know for certain that there is no internal injuries. Hopefully she will be well enough to leave her bed tomorrow, all being well. Dr Woods will be in later to check on her, in the meantime, the nurses can reach either him, or my Father, if you require.

Dad stood with his back to Ben, acknowledging his words with only a brief nod. Ben looked at me over Dad's shoulder and winked. It was all I could do not to laugh at the quirky expression on his face. At that Ben disappeared, closing the door quietly behind him. A few seconds later, I thought I heard another door close just as gently and wondered if that was the door to his room.

Apprehensively I looked at my father, who was pacing the area of the room, obviously still annoyed about something. I waited, knowing that sooner or later he would tell me what was on his mind but avoided asking all the same. I really didn't have the energy for any kind of confrontation this morning. After several minutes, he finally came towards the bed.

"I can't believe they wouldn't let you take your tablet now, even when they knew you had missed it yesterday," he grumbled. I just looked at him, completely bemused. No "How are you today Leah? Are you in any pain? How was the journey? Did it hurt much with all the movement?" Just a ridiculous rant about stupid vitamins. Still not wanting an argument, I smiled weakly at him, hoping he would move on quickly.

He sat on the chair that Ben had recently vacated and looked at me. Watching him now, it felt as though he didn't care for me at all. Was I really that much of a bind to him? He stared at me in silence for a very long time. I could see him weighing something up in his mind but I had no idea what it was.

Suddenly he was back by my side, gripping my lower arm. I tried hard not to wince with the pain of his grip, which was tightening quickly and pressing on my bruises.

"Leah, I don't care what this *boy* is to you, you are to have nothing more to do with him from the minute you leave this room, do you understand?" His grip tightened when I didn't answer and I stifled a groan. "Leah?"

I looked at him, how could I promise to have nothing to do with the man I had fallen in love with? How could *my Dad* even expect that of me? Surely he wanted what was best for me and being with Ben was that. Why couldn't he see that? Of course I had absolutely no idea how Ben felt about me but that was beside the point.

By this time, Dad's hand was really hurting my arm and I looked up at him, suddenly frightened again. Didn't he realise how much this would hurt?

Despite the pain, I was not going to agree to this. As unobtrusively as I could, I gently pulled at the cable for the bed remote control, gradually pulling it toward my free hand. As Dad leant over me, putting his weight through the hand clutching my arm, I finally got it to me and managed to press the red call button.

Within seconds the attractive nurse was back in the room.

"Mr Clinton, what **on earth** do you think you are doing? Let go of her **at once,** do I need to remind you of what I said outside?" Her quiet air of authority impressed me but she would be no match for my father. "Mr Clinton, let go right now, or I will keep to my word and have you permanently removed from this hospital, I **will not** ask you again."

His hand closed even tighter around my arm and I closed my eyes against the pain, trying to ignore the urge to cry out. The nurse pressed a discreet button on the wall of my room and within seconds I heard the door open again.

"Mr Clinton, this is your last chance to let go of Leah **now**," she stated, her voice steely and calm with authority. My father paid no attention to her, so she turned to the two security guards that had entered my room. "Please ensure that Mr Clinton is escorted out immediately and off the premises. He is not allowed to return to this room, or the grounds, again unless it is specifically requested by Miss Clinton. Notify the gatehouse of my instructions and that they are to refuse him entry, I will follow it up with the required forms," she instructed clearly. What kind of hospital needed this level of security, I wondered? It was to no avail though, as Dad still refused to let go. The guards looked at the nurse, who glanced around the room again, took a deep breath and then turned and knocked loudly twice on the hidden door in the archway.

Before I could take it all in, Ben was through the door and by my father's side, grabbing the arm that held me down.

"Mr Clinton, I know you have been asked to let go of Leah and asked to leave, I suggest you do so now before this gets any worse. I will not stand by and watch Leah get hurt, **do you understand**?"

The two men looked at each other for a long moment, fury boiling in one man's eyes, determination in the other. Without another word to anyone and not even a glance my way, my father suddenly let go and turned to leave the room. The security guards flanked him on either side and escorted him away without another word being said.

I collapsed back onto my bed, my arm throbbing where he had held so tightly and tears began streaming down my face, defying my desperation to hide my dismay. Ben was by my side, gently wiping the tears away, whilst the nurse gently lifted the sleeve of my shirt. I winced at the movement and watched her face as she pursed her lips, shaking her head. Glancing up she caught my eyes and looked away embarrassed. Quietly she set about putting an ice pack onto this latest injury, strapping cloth over and under the cold to protect my skin.

With only the slightest acknowledgment of us both she left the room, closing the door quietly behind her and we were suddenly alone.

Despite this, I couldn't stop the tears and I turned away, badly wanting Ben not to see me like this. To my surprise he gently took my chin and turned my face back to him, leaning towards me and looking down into my eyes.

"Leah, we can't let this carry on, next time he could do some real damage to you, or worse. You are not going back to that cottage again until this is completely sorted out, it just isn't safe." He rattled through the sentence, as though trying to get his point across before I argued. I lay there, looking up at him, tears still streaming down my cheeks. What was I going to say? Should I admit that I was now terrified of being alone in a hospital room with my own father, let alone the cottage that was supposed to be my home?

How was I going to make Ben understand that this was not the man of my childhood, the loving, playful father that had taken me for long walks alongside the canal to feed the ducks, pretending to throw me in when the crumbs were gone. The man I had idolised all my life, the one that had been my anchor after Mom. The vicious, violent man that had just been thrown out of my hospital room bore absolutely no resemblance to the man I remembered, he was now a complete stranger to me.

Looking into my eyes, Ben smiled very gently, reached down and took my hand. He brought it very slowly up towards him and before I really took in what was happening, he gently kissed it. My nerves tingled with the feel of his kiss and I longed to be closer to him, to have him hold me while I wept.

"Leah, please don't worry, I will be right here for you, we will sort this out together. You are not on your own now."

As he let go of my hand, I struggled, trying desperately to sit up properly but the pain in my arm from earlier made it impossible. To my embarrassment, Ben was there, beside me, sliding his arm behind my back and lifting me with seemingly very little effort.

"I mean it Leah, you can't go back there. It is just too dangerous. If he can be like that with you when in a place like this, I dread to think what he could do if you were on your own. I'll speak to my Father about you coming to stay with us, we have plenty of room and you'd get on really well with my sister, Anna. It would give Mom someone else to fuss over too."

Despite the thrill that shot through me at his words, I shook my head. "No, Ben, I couldn't do that. What would people say? It just wouldn't be right." Realising what I had said I quickly looked up at him, embarrassed. Had I given too much about my feelings away?

For a brief moment he looked deflated and my heart leaped. Then he slowly nodded, "I suppose you're right but we need to do something, you still can't go back there. I'm pretty sure my Father will have some good ideas." He turned his eyes away, thinking carefully. I lay there watching him. The thought of sharing a house with him, although tempting on one level, was scary, there would be no way that I could keep my feelings to myself twenty four seven.

"Leah, I'm just going to go and make a few phone calls. Why don't you rest, I won't be long," he said, squeezing my arm gently and then quickly leaving the room.

I closed my eyes. Suddenly I was very tired, of everything. I didn't want to have to think or talk, I just wanted to slip away and sleep until everything had gone away. This just wasn't like me. I never used to run away from my problems.

Making Plans

Another dream free night passed, although I couldn't really say I had rested well. Dr Woods had been to see me when he arrived but I'm embarrassed to admit that I pretended to be asleep rather than having to make polite conversation. Throughout the day I'd heard low murmurs outside my room and assumed that he had caught up with Ben and would now know all about yesterday's trouble on top of everything else. Ben hadn't mentioned it when he had been in to see me but other than him, I just didn't want to have to face anyone at the moment.

As the fog of sleep started to lift, I noticed the array of flowers around the room – strange I hadn't noticed them being brought in – I wondered who they were from, although I could probably hazard a guess. I flexed my back slightly, wondering whether I would finally be up to moving today. The pain shot through me and I cringed, although I was surprised how much movement I now had. This helped brighten my spirits slightly and I slowly struggled through the pain and managed to get myself out of bed and over to the closet. I rummaged through the new clothing hanging there and made my way slowly over to the bathroom to freshen up. Three days of hospital beds and nurses having to do everything for me, had left me feeling grungier than ever.

Taking my time against the pain and still limited mobility, I slowly managed to wash, brush my hair and change. Although I longed for a shower, I knew that I was not up to climbing in and out of the bath and there was no way I was going to ask for anyone to help me do that. The little I had managed to do however helped and I felt much better for having a little more independence and being in fresh clean clothes.

During this slow process I thought through what had happened recently and finally resolved not to dwell on the happenings of the last day that I had seen my Dad. As a fresher at the University, I was entitled to student accommodation on site, so I would make contact with the Bursar as soon as possible and find out what was still available. That decision made, I gently brushed my hair back into the customary ponytail and looked at myself in the mirror critically. I had certainly never been good looking but now I looked like death warmed up. I smiled, that had always been one of Mom's expressions for when I was poorly as a child. My skin was sallow and there were large, purplish bruises around my eyes, which were sunken into my face. Despite escaping more serious injury, the accident had certainly taken its toll on me. Awkwardly I brushed my fringe forward, trying to improve my gaunt appearance at least a little, that was really the best I could manage, so it would have to do for now.

Wandering back into my room, I decided not to go back to the bed and instead made my way into the lounge area. Sitting on the chaise longue, I was surprised by just how comfortable it really was. Leaning back I started to flick through the channels on the TV, desperately looking for something to watch to relieve the boredom. This place is really more like a fancy hotel I thought to myself as I flicked through the "on tap" movies and glanced quickly at the "pay per view" listing. This place must be costing Ben's family a fortune as it was, without me adding additional costs such as films to it.

I glanced at the clock several times over the next few hours. Ben hadn't been in to see me and I was reluctant to ask the ever changing nurses who came to check on me and top up my medication. I didn't want to sound too desperate but in the previous days since the accident, he had always at least popped in to say hello by now.

It was almost lunchtime by the time the door between our rooms was finally thrown open and Ben bounced into the room. I knew immediately something was up, he was positively glowing.

"You are not going to believe this!" he said as he rushed over to me.

"We've been asked to play at Symphony Hall, in the regional finals, to represent Warwickshire!"

Without thinking he pulled me up into his arms and swung me around. I gasped in surprise and he hesitated, worry flashing across his forehead.

"Sorry, did I hurt you?" he asked, pulling back slightly, suddenly full of remorse.

"Not at all," I lied, not wanting him to let go, despite the pain that was coursing through me at the movement. I smiled up at him, feeling the excitement that was coursing through him. "What? How?" I asked, annoyed at my inability to speak coherently. Being this close to him was having an adverse effect on my mind.

"We entered a competition a couple of months ago. It was before we met," he added quickly, almost apologetically. "We had to send in a demo tape. It was done as a bit of a joke really, we never honestly thought we would stand a chance of being chosen but it was. We'd been sent application forms following a gig we did at the Students' Union at the end of last term. Anyway, apparently the judges loved "Chasing the Sunset," so they want us to play that, plus one other, at the regional finals!"

He pulled me closer to him in his excitement. A lump caught in my throat as I looked up at him, this was what I had been waiting for, had longed for, to be this close to him. If I was honest though, I had absolutely no idea what to do next. The silence stretched between us as Ben gazed down into my face.

"You are so beautiful," he whispered and before I got chance to say anything to disagree, his mouth had found mine and we started to kiss. Tenderly, at first and then it became more insistent, the passion building as his lips parted mine, twisting my mouth with his urgency. The fluttering in my stomach grew stronger, making my head spin and I felt as though I would collapse in a heap if Ben had let go.

It felt like an age had passed when things started to slow and we finally separated, our breathing still coming rapidly. The room swirled as I gazed up into Ben's face and for that moment I really believed that nothing else in world mattered. As the reality of what had happened started to creep in to my consciousness, my cheeks flushed with embarrassment and I looked away from him, scared that somehow I had made him do something he hadn't wanted to do. Gently Ben cupped my chin in his hand and brought my face back to him, gazing into my eyes, then, as if to answer my thoughts, he tenderly kissed me again.

His hand lingered on my neck as for a few moments we just stared at one another, soaking one another in. I have no way of knowing what he was thinking but my mind was a mess, odd single word thoughts trying to make sense of the feelings that had awakened inside me.

Suddenly Ben spoke, breaking the silence between us. "I've wanted to kiss you almost since the first time I caught sight of you but I was never sure how **you** felt, you seemed to give off such mixed signals and I didn't want to frighten you away." His eyes searched mine, as though he could read his answer from them. "Please Leah, say something; I need to understand how you feel, about this… and about me."

I looked up at him, wondering how to even begin. My thoughts spun as I tried to work out for myself the thoughts and feelings that were surging through me as I began to recover.

"I don't know where to begin," I muttered and his face fell as he stepped away from me slightly. "No, Ben, it's not like that, please... I just can't find the right words to explain, even to myself. I've never felt anything like this before, even with Greg and I've told you what happened there. It kind of feels... as though... my whole life had been leading to this one single moment." I shook my head slowly. I still wasn't making any sense.

"I've realised over the last couple of days that I've started to develop feelings for you but I was trying to reason with myself. I just can't understand why someone as wonderful as you would be interested in a nothing like me. Even now, after... it still just doesn't make any sense."

He shook his head slowly, frustration evident on his face.

"Leah, you are the most perfect person I have ever met. It's not just about your looks and for once believe me when I say you are beautiful, it is everything about you," he continued as I started to disagree with him, "I don't care how little you think of yourself, I've never met anyone like you, or who makes me feel the way I do when we are together. It's as if I am suddenly whole again."

I leaned forward, my head resting against his chest, not wanting him to see the strength of my feelings in my face. I suddenly felt very scared, of losing him or worse still, that this would turn out to be just another one of my vivid dreams. None of this made any sense, he was such a wonderful man, why on earth would he want someone as ordinary as me, when he could undoubtedly choose any woman he wanted?

He held me gently, with his arms wrapped around me, holding me close but without making me feel trapped. Not that I would. I wanted to stay there, safe in this refuge. Nothing could hurt me when I was here with him.

I don't know how long we stood like that, close together, almost as one, talking quietly, sharing stories and memories and kisses. My whole body began to ache with the effort of standing so long and I became more and more conscious of how much I was physically leaning on Ben, to relieve the pain as much as needing to be close to him. Without my needing to say anything however, he gently led me to the chaise longue, where we sat together, his arms still wrapped around me as I leant into him. The relief from standing was almost immediate and we continued to talk gently, occasionally stealing gentle kisses, content in being together.

Most of what Ben told me was trivial, the odd childhood memory and a little about his family. I now knew his father was called Joe, his mother Eloise and he had a younger sister, Anna, who by the sounds of it was only about a year younger than him. He lit up when the conversation turned to his music, how he felt when he was writing or playing. I told him everything and anything that came into my befuddled brain, most of it didn't really make sense and I even talked about Mom for the first time since she went. Ben seemed to understand what I was trying to tell him, even though I wasn't sure myself. I don't remember the nurses coming and going but they must have done at some point, because I slowly became aware of the sedating effect of the medication again.

I looked up at Ben and smiled, I'm pretty sure it must have looked a bit lopsided because I felt kind of wobbly and then I finally drifted off to sleep, still leaning against him.

Poisoned

I never expected the dream this time, I had already gone several days without it and right here, right now, I felt safer than ever, one of **those** dreams was the last thing on my mind...

"Leah, stay where you are!" the voice shouted, above the chaos that surrounded me. People were milling everywhere. This time my surroundings were familiar, it was the castle grounds again but despite there being a lot of people, I still felt very alone. I could hear the little girl crying out again but this time couldn't work out where she was in order to be able to help her. That awful noise was getting louder again and every muscle in my body hurt, even though I was currently standing still.

This time I heard the car before it pulled up. I was back at the entrance to the castle grounds and the engine grew louder and louder as it headed towards me. It was the same car, there was no doubt about that but this time I was reluctant to get in, scared about what I might find. This time however as *the door opened, that same voice called to me from inside, "Come on Leah, jump, there is no time to waste!" As it called, that horrible roaring sound was almost upon me and I jumped in, feeling that there was really no other option open to me. As I slammed the door behind me, my eyes focussed on the little girl that had been calling for her Daddy and as she turned towards the noise of the car, her face registered in my unconscious mind. It was me!*

I didn't have time to dwell any further on it, as the car headed away from the castle. I strained and strained until I could no longer make out the little girl in the shadows and then eventually gave in to the arm that was trying to pull me closer. Trembling with a mixture of shock and fear, I allowed myself to be drawn closer, gaining comfort in the familiar scent and shape of the body that held me. As I drifted off, those all too familiar voices were talking again. I wish I had the strength to listen, to really understand what it was they were saying. Perhaps then these dreams would actually make some sense. The crash made me jump and as I opened my eyes, I realised

that the car window had been smashed and a long,
angular, fleshless arm was reaching toward me…

I bolted upright, mind still foggy from the
dream, for an instant fighting against the arms that
held me, unsure of where I was and what had got me.

"Shhh, Leah, its ok, I'm here, nothing is going
to hurt you now. Quiet now, you're safe."

That voice… Was it the same one from my
dream? Was I still asleep? Just as those thoughts
entered my mind however, reality started to seep in
and Ben was sitting up next to me, trying to hold me
close and soothe me. I relaxed back into him, glad to
be safe again.

"Leah, what was it? Was it something I said or
did?" he asked, gently rubbing my back and holding
me as close as I would let him. I shook my head
sadly, how could I explain this absurdity to him
when I still couldn't explain it to myself? It was sure
to bring him crashing to his senses about me and go
running for the hills as fast as he could get away.

I didn't really get a chance though, as he suddenly asked:

"What was it about the girl, Leah? You kept mentioning her and then suddenly said something about her being "me." Please, Leah, tell me what was happening, I might be able to help you make some sense of it all."

I shook my head slowly. "Trust your instincts," Mom had said in my dreams and every bone in my body told me to trust Ben, that we were meant to be together and nothing like this would frighten him off. But in my waking mind, I was terrified of making him think I was mad and driving him away.

Again he was rubbing my back, gently and reassuringly. "Leah, we all have bad dreams and they are nothing to be ashamed of, particularly after all you have been through. Please, trust me, I won't be running off anywhere, I promise."

I looked at him, slightly startled, how did he know what I was thinking? His smile won me over. "Leah, I would be thinking that right now in your shoes but please believe me, I have waited a very long time to find you and a few bad dreams, even if they are a little odd, are not going to frighten me off, not now."

I smiled hesitantly. I knew what he meant. I felt as though I had been waiting my whole life for him too, to make me a whole person, not just the sum of several parts. Slowly, hesitantly at first, I started to describe the dreams – the car, the noises, the little girl and the location, finally mentioning the familiar voices.

As I told him, he held me close, saying nothing but telling me everything I needed to hear by the way he held and comforted me. Suddenly I was irritated with myself for not trusting him sooner. I should have known he would understand and not think that I had completely lost my senses. What was it that Mom had always said to me? "Trust your instincts Leah, they will never steer you wrong."

Right from the first time we met, my instincts had guided me to trust Ben and I was stupid for not letting them steer me. I felt as though so much time had been wasted, even though it was really only a few weeks.

As we sat there, sometimes talking, sometimes just relaxing in the comfortable silence around us, a new sense of peacefulness came over me. Despite being in a hospital room, I felt whole, complete and I finally allowed myself to admit that I had fallen completely and utterly in love with this man and it felt right.

Ben looked down at me, deep in thought and smiled gently at me as he leaned forward and kissed my cheek. "Leah, it is so wonderful to see you like this but there is still a lot that you need to know and I won't rest until you understand **everything**." I looked up at him, still floating in the depths in his eyes and my feelings for him.

"Ben, there isn't anything that you could tell me, anything that I could learn, that could change the way I feel right now," I began but I didn't get time to go further, as Dr Woods came into the room.

Suddenly I was concerned, his expression spoke volumes and I knew that whatever he had come to say, he had wrestled with himself before entering the room. Instinctively I tensed, fearing the unknown and I felt Ben's arm tighten protectively around me.

"What is it?" I asked, sudden fear shaking my voice.

"Leah, how do you feel, **right now** and is anything different since before the accident?" he began, slowly.

I looked back at him, puzzled. There had been nothing wrong with me before the accident, so why would there be a specific difference now? He must have meant since the accident, not since before I decided.

"Well, I've got more movement now, or at least it doesn't hurt as much to move…" I began but he shook his head, interrupting me.

"No, Leah, I meant compared to how you felt before the accident, I am well aware of the injuries you sustained and your progress in recovering from those."

"I… I'm sorry, I don't understand what you mean," I finally stuttered, completely confused and looking towards Ben for an explanation. The expression on his face jolted me. It was as if he already understood what Dr Woods was trying to say.

"Ben…" I began and he turned those eyes towards me, full of concern but there was a shadow there, concealing something.

I stopped. There was something different, something that had almost crept up on me. If they hadn't have pushed, I probably would not have even noticed; but how could I begin to explain, to put it into words?

"Try Leah, just tell me, no-one is judging you here," my mother's voice crept into my mind, recalling one of many conversations that we had had, when I had tried to explain myself and my arguments with my friends. "If you don't understand yourself, how can you expect them to?" She would often say.

"It's as if something has lifted," I began, hesitant, embarrassed at first, I hated being the centre of attention at the best of times, let alone explaining myself.

"For a few years now, even before we moved, I've felt trapped, enclosed by everything that has happened, unable to let anyone in close to me and share how I was feeling – even my Dad."

Ben's arms tightened around me as I said it but I was afraid to look at him, to try to determine what he was thinking.

"I suppose since the accident and… what happened. I've begun to feel more like my old self. More willing to share, to… feel, it's the only way I can put it"

Dr Woods nodded thoughtfully, as though that helped explain things. "And since the accident and your move here Leah, you've been telling the nurses about these headaches. Can you explain them to me a little more? Where are they, what does it feel like and things like that if you can, please?"

I stopped for a minute. "It has felt like someone had my head in a vice. Those first few days, it was as though they were squeezing it tighter and tighter, so much so that even thinking hurt at times, as though the thought processes themselves were causing pain as they triggered across my head." I shook myself, frustrated at my inability to describe it properly.

"I have to admit, at one stage I thought I was going to have to ask you to sedate me, something to get me away from the pain but suddenly, I think yesterday afternoon maybe evening it started to lift, as though those connections were starting to repair themselves. Then, today, they have been a lot better, or they seem to be – unless that is partly to do with what has happened."

I looked at Ben quickly, then away again. I could feel the heat rushing through my face. He took my hand gently, stroking the side of my thumb with his.

"What is all of this about, please tell me. There's something seriously wrong isn't there, something you've discovered following the accident?" I asked. Without looking at him I sensed the change in Ben's expression, what was it he was waiting for?

"Leah, can you tell me please, where **did** your vitamins come from?" Dr Woods asked. "Why do you take them?"

I looked at him, still confused, why bring those stupid things up now? "Dad got them for me a few years ago; I suppose it wasn't long after Mom… He said he would try to do the best he could and look after me in the way that Mom had. Then he said that he was no match for her skills in the kitchen, so would I please take the vitamins to counteract what might occasionally be a very unbalanced diet. I don't understand, it was only vitamins…" I stopped, Dr Woods expression told me differently.

"I'm sorry Leah, I can't really explain but these things are most definitely **not** vitamins. There are a couple of the compounds contained in them that our lab has been unable to identify but I can tell you they contained unusual supplements. There is a behaviour suppressant similar to Ritalin, as well as two additional compounds. I'm sorry if you feel that I am interfering but it is my policy to never take unidentified medication at face value. I had them tested before I would let you take them alongside what I have prescribed, I couldn't account for the consequences otherwise."

I stared at him with what must have been an extremely stupid look on my face, completely confused.

"You must have got them mixed up in the lab. I've not been taking anything but vitamins..." I stopped as Dr Woods shook his head.

"I'm sorry Leah, there's no mistake. The tablets you have been taking are most definitely not vitamins. Can you tell me please why you have been taking them?"

I shook my head in bewilderment, suddenly everything was closing in around me and I didn't understand what was going on. All of a sudden I felt very small and insecure, like a child on her first day at school. "Tell the truth Leah, you have nothing to be frightened of if you always tell the truth," said Mom's voice in my mind. It was as if she was right there with me in the room.

"I'm sorry, I really don't understand. I've never even bought these things, Dad always..." Finally the realisation of what was being implied began to dawn and as it did so I became conscious that Ben had already got there ahead of me, as his arms were tighter than ever and his face had frozen somewhere between anger and disbelief.

"But... it just doesn't make any sense... why on earth would..." I stumbled over my words, not even sure what it was I was trying to say.

As I searched frantically for some kind of logical explanation, I felt Ben stir, releasing his grip and moving from underneath me. As I turned to look at him he was already starting to stand. He gazed wordlessly at me for a moment, then, without saying anything either to me or Dr Woods, he left the room. A few seconds later I heard a huge crash, a muttered curse and another crash and it dawned on me that it was Ben I could hear.

As though in a daze I looked back at Dr Woods, my questions undoubtedly written all over my face and he half smiled, a gentle look on his face.

"Leah, I can't give you the reasons why but it is fairly obvious that these tablets have been provided for a very specific reason. Whilst I am unable to specify the exact reason you have been prescribed them, I can tell you that the contents that we have been able to identify are behavioural and memory suppressants. For whatever reason, whoever prescribed these tablets wants to control your mind, probably to ensure you don't remember someone or something."

I watched him, my mind completely numb, trying to make sense of what he was explaining to me. The last thing I remember is shaking my head, as though trying to make the pieces come together and the room starting to spin around me. I heard Dr Woods shout for help, alongside my own more distant voice calling for Ben at the same time; then I felt someone catch me as I slipped off the chaise and crashed to the floor.

The next few days were a blur. Suddenly I was confined to bed again and my abdomen was extremely sore. Many doctors and nurses arrived and then fading away again, injecting something into the drip that had somehow reappeared and then long periods of stillness, complete blackness where the only relief was the very occasional sound of Ben's voice, talking to me gently, telling me that everything would be ok. I could only catch part of what he was saying, as I drifted in and out of consciousness but I caught the words "ruptured spleen" and "accident", the rest is unknown.

Escape

The roar was back again, this time sounding as though it were right on top of me. The familiar smell of burnt rubber followed. This time I knew that these dreams weren't just nightmares, they were trying to tell me something but I couldn't work out what. Every time I got close to even understanding what was after me, I woke up, soaked through and frightened to death. Somehow this time I needed to stick with it, to allow the dream to continue. It was my only hope of getting rid of them once and for all.

My thought process was interrupted by the now commonplace squeal of brakes. I turned just as that familiar black car screeched to a halt, the door flying open. Again, the same voice called to me – should I jump in, or wait to see if I could finally find out what happened.

"Leah, now, I can't save you if you don't come NOW!" the voice yelled. Throwing hesitation aside, I jumped in, an arm grabbing me and pulling me into the car. My hesitation though had caused a change in the storyline, those unnatural yellow eyes were *upon us and I could hear the Harbinger scrabbling at the door of the car as we pulled away. I shrank back into the car, trying not to let the fear get the better of me. I needed to finally understand what this was all about.*

Despite my resolve, I found myself waking, once again soaked through. Frustrated, I tried to turn myself over, angry that I hadn't had the strength to force my way through the fear and discover whatever it was that they were trying to tell me. I winced as I caught my left ribs, which must be from the surgery I recalled Ben telling me about. Annoyed and determined to have some success I tried rolling onto my right side, which felt a little easier. As my eyes focussed in the changing light, I started to make out a moving silhouette in the lounge area of my room heading towards my bed and as it came into focus, fear rose in my throat, as understanding dawned on my fragile consciousness that the figure was not Ben, nor did it appear human.

Panic hit me as it felt as though the blood drained slowly from my body. Frantically I sought for help, an object to throw, even the alarm, anything to help rescue me from this life form in my room. My mind watched in ice cold fear as the figure changed, from the angular fleshless omens of my dreams, to a more familiar, more human shape. I watched nervously, was it really still just a dream?

It moved closer, transforming into a man wearing what seemed to be normal jeans and a shirt. My frozen brain shuddered, fighting to identify the somehow familiar shape as it approached but I still couldn't place it.

I cowered back into the bed, desperate for it to absorb me, protect me from what was coming. As my brain struggled to make sense and accept the still shifting form, I gasped. It was holding a large syringe filled with a bright blue, almost azure coloured, liquid. I struggled further, trying to scream, to get attention somehow but no sound would come and I watched helpless as the figure injected the entire contents into my drip. I struggled to memorise the face, understand who would do this to me but I wasn't strong enough to fight and I drifted away.

The next few days were more than a bit of a blur. I surfaced from unconsciousness for seconds at a time, only to see faceless uniforms and bodies moving around my room. I remember hearing Dr Woods and a few familiar nurses' voices but they were low and muffled and I stood no chance of comprehending even if I had heard them clearly. I also knew my Dad had tried to visit, I vaguely remember him trying to rip the drip from my hand and take me home. Once more, hospital security had arrived and he had been thrown out. I recall hearing his raised, angry voice swiftly joined by other, equally insistent but somehow less abrasive voices and the sound of slamming doors. Other than that I drifted in and out of consciousness for what seemed like seconds at a time, aware of nurses and other visitors coming and going, following their normal routines but other than that I was adrift in the fog.

I have no idea what day or even week it was when I finally awoke properly. I lay there dazed, trying to simply work out what time of day it was. There was no sound or movement from outside my room, although the light peeking through the blinds told me that it must at least be daylight hours. I lay there for a few seconds allowing my brain to start to focus, half expecting to drift away once more. I stirred slightly, as the realisation dawned that for once, I didn't feel groggy, or ache to return to the numbness of sleep. Slowly I became accustomed to the feeling and as it did so my mind started to absorb and then analyse the scene around me. Something about the room was different but what was it? I gazed around the room. The flowers and furniture all looked the same... so what was it...? As I continued to take in the scene around me, I realised that all of the medical equipment had disappeared, even the monitors. My heart lurched, that meant that the thing couldn't return and inject more of that stuff into me.

I jumped as the door opened and I spun my head with a huge smile on my face, fully expecting it to be Ben. My smile froze as I absorbed the figure of

Dr Woods as he strode into the room, although I tried desperately to hide my disappointment.

He smiled gently as he noted the change in my mood.

"Well, young lady, it is very nice to see you wide awake again, that was quite a turn you took and you had us quite concerned."

I smiled hesitantly, wondering how much he actually knew about what had happened. My brain searched the memories trying to identify the face that had been in my room, although I still couldn't say who it was, I started to relax. It most definitely was not Dr Woods.

He glanced quickly around the room. "Leah, we've had to move you from your previous suite…" He noted my alarm and quickly added, "No, it's ok, you're still at The Chase but we know that your room was broken into and we are concerned about your Father's behaviour, therefore we have moved you, with the Clinton's permission, in order to protect you." He paused for a moment, watching me carefully. As he spoke I had turned my head away, fighting to control the tears that threatened to come, desperate to understand where I could go from here.

The realisation lay heavily on me. I was completely on my own at nineteen, with no family, not even a close relative to offer advice, guidance, or to drop by for a chat about old times. Suddenly I felt extremely alone – the idea of having no-one close, no-one with any of knowledge of my history or even my heritage around might sound tempting but the reality is a terrible thing.

"Leah, it's ok, you don't need to worry. I would like to keep an eye on you for another few days at least. I need to be confident that you have recovered from the splenectomy but also that your system is completely clean from *those* drugs and you are fully recovered from the accident. I know Ben has been making plans for when you are discharged, so I am sure things will not seem as difficult as they do right now." He smiled gently and I turned back towards him, nodding my understanding, still unable to trust myself to speak. He lingered for a moment then left as quietly as he had entered.

Once more I was alone but I was no longer at peace. What was I going to do? Term would start shortly and I was pretty sure that the decent student accommodation would be gone by now. On top of that all of my books, clothes, music, laptop etc. were at home and in the current circumstances, it wasn't exactly going to be easy to retrieve them. This meant that I did not have easy access to any of the documentation I would need to secure student accommodation.

I lay there, head turned towards the window, silent tears coursing down my face. I've never been one for crying and self-pity, as it is generally pointless but in my current predicament and in full realisation of my isolated state, there was nothing that I could do to stop the tears.

I'm not sure how long I lay like that, alone with my thoughts but as I did the shadows in my room changed as the day drew on.

"Stop this right now Leah." I heard my mother's voice. "Maudlin won't help you right now. Get yourself up out of bed and freshen yourself up my girl, you'll feel much better for it and then we can start to make some real plans." I smiled through the tears. That was just her way; don't dwell on the bad things. Focus on the future and moving forward. How strange it was that even now I could hear her say these things, knowing exactly what it would take to get me back on track.

Carefully I lowered the bed and climbed out. My legs ached from lack of use but at least the movement caused little real pain. Slowly I hobbled towards the bathroom, my steps easing as my muscles stopped complaining and finally accepted the movements needed to restore their normal rhythms.

Gingerly I showered and changed. I have no idea how long it took me, I was simply conscious that every new movement brought a twinge of complaint from my body, complaint about being used for the first time in so many days, along with recovery from the injuries. Despite everything that had happened, I still knew that I had got off lightly in the accident, although the ruptured spleen was now added to the list, a few broken ribs, a broken collarbone and severe cuts and bruising was still lucky. Working through the minor challenges that recovery created, I started to get changed and a plan began to take shape. I worked through it step by step, thinking through all the stages until I was satisfied that it was achievable. Now all I needed to do was decide when.

I glanced at the clock and was delighted to see that it was still only mid-afternoon – 3:21 pm to be precise. My father would undoubtedly still be at the office; therefore if I could get to the cottage, I stood a fair chance of reclaiming at least some of my possessions before he got home. Encouraged by this thought I hurried to finish dressing and drying my hair, wincing at the pain this caused, while trying desperately not to overanalyse my appearance in the mirror.

There was no time to leave a note for Ben… "I'll be back quickly enough," I thought to myself, I'll be back long before he starts to really worry. Without stopping to think things through any further,

I opened the fire door to my room and stepped through. Thank goodness for ground floor rooms, I thought, at least this way I wouldn't have to answer any awkward questions, or explain myself to the nursing staff.

I walked as quickly as I could down the side of the wall, thankful that there were so few windows that I needed to duck under. I shivered as I went, the weather was still pretty lousy and the sky looked as though it could bring yet another storm at any moment. I picked up the pace as swiftly as my aching limbs would allow, determined to find my way to the cottage as fast as I could and retrieve my belongings before the heavens opened and drenched me once more.

"Leah, be careful."

I jumped at the sound and instinctively glanced around me. "Don't be so stupid," I reprimanded myself, "You know that she's not really here, it's just your mind playing tricks again." Still annoyed with myself I stormed forward. As I rounded the corner of the building I came to an abrupt halt, shocked by what lay before me.

I knew that The Chase was exclusive but I hadn't realised quite how secure the site was. Large wrought iron gates secured the long driveway and along the boundary lines were huge trees, from where I stood I could make out evergreen Eucalyptus and fir trees, alongside the more traditional English deciduous silver birch, yew and copper beech trees. The rich, dense foliage made the surroundings extremely peaceful and secluded but I could also make out secure metal fencing marking the boundary. How on earth was I going to be able to get out of here without being noticed?

My heart started to race as my mind searched for a solution but as it did, something started to knock on the door of my consciousness. I sought out a plan, trying to ignore the nagging doubt but eventually, it forced its way through. Although I had never been a patient here, I vaguely remembered The Chase from a visit my Dad had made to an older colleague here. He'd insisted that I come with him, so that we could go on somewhere for something to eat but I'd stayed in the car.

As I started to remember, alarm began to take reign. The Chase was set in the grounds of an old Victorian mansion, with the old house still forming part of the property, which had been extended beyond all recognition. The entrance did not have this long driveway, nor did it have the plethora of trees that I had just admired. Where the hell was I?

My legs began to weaken as panic tore through me. Where had I been moved to and how on earth was I going to find my way back to the Cottage to reclaim my things?

I desperately needed to get my stuff and be able to take the short time I had left at The Chase to plan for my future. I knew I wasn't strong enough to face my father alone, so it needed to be done now, while he would be at work. But where was I and how could I get to the cottage from here?

I took a deep breath to clear my head but as I did so the world started to spin as though I were on board on a ship in a force six storm. I staggered slightly, straight into the arms of the man that had crept up behind me. I tried to scream before my brain recognised his uniform as being one of the guards here. He caught me with a curse as I collapsed, blacking out once more.

Solutions

The car door slammed behind me. The Harbinger's long claws reached through the broken window scratching at my arm as it tried to grab me and pull me away. It uttered a horrendous yowl as the car accelerated away, throwing it onto the pathway. As I watched in horror, it leapt to its feet and tore after us, quickly joined by another.

"Leah it will be ok, we just need to get you away from here and then we will all be fine." That gorgeous, silky voice came from the front of the car. Unable to stop myself I reached forward, desperate to touch the person it came from once more. My heart ached with the longing.

"Watch out!" The voice came from the man holding me; he grabbed me and held on tight. I heard the squealing of brakes, the scrabbling of tyres as they fought to come to a standstill and a scream. I was suddenly flying through mid-air, crashing into the seat in front of me. The man that had been holding me continued his journey, between the two front seats of the car and a few seconds later I heard

glass shattering, just as I began to ricochet back onto
the rear seat of the car with a huge jolt. Grinding
metal complained as it was forced to stop instantly,
in spite of the speed we had been travelling and my
head bounced off the headrest of the seat. Finally the
crescendo of noise ceased and I was left with nothing
but silence. Absolute silence.

As I struggled to make sense of what had just
happened, the door of the car was ripped open and
the same long fleshless arm, with its huge claws,
reached in, grabbed me and started to drag me out of
the car.

I bolted awake. Heart racing my eyes scoured the room, looking for something, some clue as to where I was and what was happening.

There was no doubting that the dreams were getting worse but at least they were progressing, although I admit I didn't like where they were going.

I struggled to sit up. Although not attached to anything, I winced as I pushed myself upright with my hands. Looking down I noticed with horror that the cannula was back. That meant I had been given something again and I was no longer sure of who, if anyone, I could trust.

I was pleased to see that I was still dressed, despite being back on the bed. Judging by the shadows only an hour had passed but with that realisation my heart sank. Even assuming we were close to home, there was no longer enough time to get to the cottage today, before my Father came home. Another day lost.

I tried to quell my fear by starting to rationalise another plan, which I could put into play first thing tomorrow, once I was familiar with time and day of the week again. If I left fairly early, it would give me longer to sort through what it was I actually needed and perhaps I would also have the time to visit the Student Accommodation offices and get something started there.

Pleased with this decision I felt my heart begin to settle. It still didn't resolve the issue of where I was now and what on earth was going on. I desperately wanted to storm out and demand explanations but somehow the little voice in my head told me to be careful, at least here I was safe, no-one had tried to harm me and I had nowhere else to go.

The weight in my stomach dropped, it was true. Even though I had no idea where I was, nor whether I was safe, I had no other choice. My mind fought against all my arguments – Ben had brought you here and he wouldn't do anything to put you in danger, would he? Everyone had been so kind and I had been well cared for and protected, surely I need not fear for my safety?

As I thought all of this through, I became aware of the dissipating storm outside. When had it started to thunder again? I vaguely recall hearing a distant rumble but not a full storm again.

The door opened and into my room strode a stranger. Tall and extremely handsome for a man of his age, he stood at what appeared to be just over six foot. With short, dark hair that was greying at the edges, he exuded a presence. Not arrogance, neither was it aggressive or snide, it was simply an aura that made you recognise his presence and accept him in a position of authority but without feeling threatened.

He smiled at me and despite my situation I found myself begin to relax. He had light blue eyes and a face that glowed when he smiled. Somehow, I felt safe.

"Hello Leah, my name is Joe Edwards – I am sorry we have to meet under these circumstances but I am Ben's father."

I felt myself blush, I could have thought of a thousand different ways in which I would have preferred to meet one of Ben's parents than this.

"Ben has had to go away for a couple of days…"

I felt my heart lurch. Where…why? How was I going to cope on my own without even Ben as my anchor. My soul ached, now I really was on my own.

A fleeting expression of surprise passed Joe's face.

"I've come to talk to you about what happens when you leave here. From what Ben and the Hospital have told me, I don't think it would be safe for you to return home right now, would you agree?"

I felt my heart sink. Despite my own acceptance of the situation, it still hurt that other people, strangers, would think like this about my Father. He had been such a fantastic Dad as I was growing up and nothing could change the love I had for him back then but I also knew that Joe was right, there was no going back now.

I nodded my agreement, the lump in my throat making me incapable of speaking.

"Leah, I don't know how much Ben has told you about our family and where we live." I shook my head in response. All I really knew is that he lived with both parents and his sister Anna, who was slightly younger, in a house close to the town centre.

"We live very close to the centre of town, in an old school house that belonged to one of my ancestors Edward de Clinton, who also started the school. We have plenty of space and I would like for you to come and stay with us until we have managed to get to the bottom of everything that has been happening." I started to object and he hurriedly continued.

"It will all be completely respectable. We have several guest rooms in the west wing of the house that are never used, so you can use a couple of those for your own needs if you would like. You are of course welcome at any time to join us in the main house but you will also have your privacy for when you require it." He paused, as though uncertain quite how to say things.

"Leah, it is obvious to me that Ben has become very close to you in what, at my age, is a very short space of time and he has told me some of what has happened to you. I don't like interfering in other people's family lives but I also could not stand by and see you alone, without any support, or see you go back home to be hurt further. You can stay as long as you like and if we manage to get to the bottom of what has been happening, you can leave at any time to go back home, as long as you feel safe to do so."

"Thank you," I stuttered, unable to think of anything else to say in the circumstances. I was truly thankful and almost giddy with relief that I had somewhere to go, where I would be safe.

"You are most welcome my dear. Ben and I retrieved your belongings, or what we thought you might need, from the Cottage when your Father was at work yesterday. I hope you don't mind but Ben took your keys from your things." I shook my head – how could I really be cross when they were trying so hard to help me and had dealt with what I knew would be the hardest part.

"When will Ben be home?" I asked, wondering how long it would be before I saw him again. For a brief second I saw Joe hesitate.

"He should be home in a few days, he's just gone away… for his music, to lay down some backing tracks for the competition," he ended in a rush, for a brief moment I saw a look of concern cross his face and the thought flashed through my mind that he wasn't telling the truth. I saw his eyes tighten as he watched me, then relax as I smiled.

"I've spoken to Dr Woods," he began again. "He would like to keep you here for another twelve hours, given this afternoon's episode, so I will send a car for you in the morning, along with Anna, my daughter and she will bring you home and help you get settled. Ben should be home by the weekend." With that he smiled again, nodded briefly and headed for the door. As he reached it, I blurted out:

"Where am I?"

He turned around slowly, "You're at The Chase, Leah. Ben told you that when you were moved here."

I watched him closely, "I know that's what he said but... when I ... went for a walk earlier," I desperately wanted to not offend this man, both because of his generosity in helping me when I had no one else but, equally as important, because of Ben.

"I don't recall The Chase having the long drive that I saw, or quite this level of... security," I continued.

He smiled slightly and then walked back towards me, perching on the end of the bed.

"Leah, The Chase is a very exclusive hospital, which caters for quite a variety of people. The normal hospital, where you would go for an appointment or as a standard patient is where you would have visited before. However if you followed the drive past the car park and continued driving, you would have ended up here, where those guests that need extra privacy can come." He glanced around as he spoke and then walked over towards the window, drawing back the voile that shielded the daylight. Pointing out of the window, he continued. "If you look closely, here, you can actually make out the corner of the hospital itself. This building, beautiful as it is, is actually the old Warwickshire Police Headquarters. They purchased the building and land two years ago when it was put up for sale." He paused, watching me closely.

"So, why was I brought to this part of the hospital?" I demanded, still very unsure of what I was being told, although the tone of my voice was far more aggressive than I intended.

Joe appeared to take it in his stride, thankfully.

"Leah, my family has been a part of this community for a very long time. We are fortunate enough to know many people and have a decent standard of living. When Ben told me what had been happening and Dr Woods called me to explain about the... difficulties that had occurred with your father, I thought it best to have you moved to somewhere that was completely safe, where there were people who could protect you if another... incident occurred. I spoke to a few people and managed to pull one or two strings. I hope that meets with your approval?" He ended the sentence with only the slightest hint of sarcasm, his mouth curved into a slight smile with one eyebrow raised as he watched me intently. His explanation seemed perfectly logical and I was eternally grateful that they were helping me like this. I quickly trawled through my knowledge of the area. Yes, there was an old mansion type building that I recalled, seemed a bit odd for a Police HQ but I do remember seeing something in the local library about them selling off an old building when I was searching for the history of the Castle.

Joe was watching me intently and I saw his eyes relax very slightly as I smiled weakly. "I'm sorry, please don't think I was being rude, I'm just so confused. So much has happened recently, that when I realised that I wasn't where I thought I had been taken, it made me anxious, that's all."

"Leah, you don't need to apologise. It hadn't occurred to us that you wouldn't know about this place, so it is our error for not being clearer with you. I'm really sorry if we caused you to worry, you really don't need anything else to bother you right now." He paused for a second. "Is there anything else you would like to ask me now, while it is just us two here?" I shook my head.

"Thank you for being open with me and I am really sorry if I came across as being abrupt or rude. I am really grateful for what you are doing for me," I said, suddenly embarrassed.

He smiled. "You are most welcome Leah, please don't worry about anything. Anna will be here tomorrow first thing to help you pack and bring you home. Actually, it occurs to me that you have never met, although knowing how close they are, I am sure Ben will have mentioned her before. Here, let me show you a recent photograph, so that you know who to expect in the morning." He quickly flicked through some photographs on his phone, "here you go, this was taken earlier in the summer, when the weather was still good." I took the phone and glanced at the picture. The girl in the picture smiled back at me. She had dark hair and the kindness I had seen in Joe also shone through her pale crystal blue eyes. I could see very little resemblance to Ben in this photograph but I suddenly felt very inadequate again, as I looked at the perfectly, if casually dressed young woman.

Joe reached for the phone. "I am sure the two of you will get along just fine," he said as he returned it to his pocket. With that, he stood up and left the room, I was alone with my thoughts and fears once more.

Breaking Through

I was back in the car, thrown against the back seat. This time I knew we had crashed, I just wasn't sure what had happened. As the shrieking of the metal subsided, I braced myself waiting for the window to shatter once more. However, this time the dream had changed. As I tried to settle my nerves and assess the scenery around me, making an attempt to establish what had happened, a figure moved in the front passenger seat. I started in surprise, I didn't remember there being a passenger. My mind struggled to make sense of the images around me. This time there was no man lying on the seat beside me, unable to stop the creature. What on earth was going on?

As I struggled to make sense of it all, the figure turned towards me. My father's face looked silently at me, scratched and bleeding from his forehead and the side of his face and he also had streaks of blood down the arm of his shirt closest to me.

"Leah, sweetheart, are you ok? Can you move?" he asked urgently. I gently flexed my limbs

and nodded silently. As I did, he turned to the body slumped forward in the driver's seat. I felt a moan escape my lips as I recognised the shape for the first time.

"Mom, Mom, wake up, are you ok?" I screamed, unable to control the fear that occupied my mind. My father shook his head urgently at me, as he gently leant towards her, stroking the hair back from her face and then pressing his forefinger and thumb against her wrist, where she still appeared to be holding the mangled steering wheel. I watched in now silent horror as he closed his eyes against his findings. Sobs silently wracked my body as I realised that my Mother was dead.

I raised my hands to my face, to wipe away the tears that were streaking down my face, as they came into view I stared blankly, unable to comprehend what my eyes were telling me. Confusion reigned as I looked at the hands in front of me; they were those of a little girl.

I woke with a start, my face wet from the tears in my sleep, body shaking. What was going on? I had been fourteen when Mom had died, not at primary school, which is the age the child appeared to be in my dream – she was maybe eight or nine years old. I lay there, still trembling, trying to make sense of things but without much luck. As my heart started to settle, I looked around me. Shadows were disappearing in the room, meaning that it must almost be morning, time to leave The Chase.

Nobody likes being in hospital but the thought of leaving this place made me more than a little apprehensive. Yes, it was a hospital but it just felt safe. Despite the intruder, I still felt safer here then I could imagine feeling elsewhere. Ben's family were being incredibly kind in taking me in like this but they would be no match for my father, if he found out where I was and turned up in one of his fits of temper. I shuddered at the thought. It was bad enough that they had seen, or heard about what had happened here, I really did not want them having to witness a scene like the one at the cottage.

The sigh that escaped said it all. I was nineteen years old, with very few options left open to me. Yes, I could go flat out and camp at the Accommodation Offices until they helped me find a place of my own but I also knew that I needed the support of someone more senior, with a bit more life experience then I currently had – although there were experiences in my life that I don't think another human being would ever share. I needed someone that I could trust and rely on – after all, what did I know about bills and stuff? Whilst we had done some money management at school, it wasn't the same. I still needed, and if I was honest, wanted, someone to confide in, someone who could offer advice, even if things seemed to be going ok.

Slowly I climbed out of bed. I wanted to be ready when Ben's sister arrived. The last thing I wanted to do was annoy this girl by keeping her waiting.

As I gingerly climbed into the shower, I allowed my mind to wander back to the dream. It just didn't make any sense. Obviously there was some truth in the dream. Mom was killed in a bad car accident, hitting a wall when she swerved to avoid a motorcyclist that lost control. She had been driving and Dad was the passenger but I was at school at the time.

Washing my hair with some difficulty, I came to the conclusion that it was just my overwrought mind trying to cope with everything that had happened. There were obviously my memories of Mom, although they had never appeared in a dream like this before. The little girl was obviously something to do with my feeling vulnerable and it was perfectly logical that Dad would feature in there too, as the Father I remember, not the way he was acting right now.

Having rough dried my hair, I wrapped the towel around my body and left the bathroom. Directly in front of me stood a young woman, standing facing the door with an expectant smile on her face. She was petite, probably only about five foot four, with elfin like features, perfect chocolate brown hair, cut in an ultra-fashionable short bob and crystal blue eyes, not quite the same shade as Ben's, although both had a sense of kindness about them. Although it had been lovely, the photograph that Joe had showed me yesterday had failed to do her justice. The differences in appearance between them all were noticeable, if it hadn't been for the mannerisms and the kindness that seemed to exude from them, you would never have placed them as family. Oblivious to my analysis, she bounded over to me, hand outstretched.

"Hi, I'm Anna. It is **so** good to meet you at last. I've been dying to come and visit you but Father thought it would be too much of an intrusion. Oh… I'm sorry, how inconsiderate of me." Her beautiful face looked mortified, as she suddenly absorbed my appearance, standing in front of her, looking like something the cat had dragged in, which was bad enough but as it stood I also only had a towel to cover my modesty.

Trying my hardest to hide my own embarrassment, I stretched out my hand. "Hello Anna, it is lovely to meet you too. I wonder if you would mind just waiting for me in the living area for a moment, so that I can tidy myself up and get dressed." She nodded silently and left the room. Trying not to be rude about it, I pushed the door to my bedroom almost too, enough to ensure she couldn't see me but not completely closed. As quickly as I could I dressed, in the jeans and shirt that had been placed there for my use, the jacket I threw over the end of the bed. Once I was satisfied that I was dressed, I opened the door between the rooms. Anna was sitting on the chaise, head back and eyes closed. Her face was completely relaxed. A stab of pure envy washed through me as I watched her. There was no other way to describe her other than beautiful. I had never seen someone more so. With very little make up, there was no tension in her face whatsoever, she simply sat there, as though meditating.

I coughed gently and her eyes flew open. With seemingly no time to adjust she sprang up off the seat.

"Leah, I am so sorry. You must think me an absolute, inconsiderate fool to come waltzing into your room like that unannounced. I should have realised that you would be getting up and dressed. Please, forgive me?" She was so contrite, I almost laughed out loud. It wasn't really as though I could take offence, given the generosity extended to me by her family and I could understand her actions, sort of. Besides, I really didn't want to make an enemy of Ben's sister.

I smiled again and held out my hands. "Please don't worry Anna, I completely understand. I should have been up and dressed much earlier than this, your Father did say that you would be here first thing." Fleetingly it flew through my mind that she also used the formal vernacular when referring to their parent. Neither she nor Ben had referred to him as Dad.

The thought was gone almost at the same instant. "Anna, why don't you join me whilst I dry off my hair and then I am more or less ready to go. Everything here belongs to The Chase, so it is only, quite literally, the things that I am standing in and my nightclothes, that we need to take with us."

She beamed at me in relief and like her father, her face lit up with that smile. Nodding happily she pulled a foldaway bag from her pocket and disappeared into the bathroom to collect the nightclothes that I'd left hanging on the back of the door. How did she know to find them there? I wondered. Then I shrugged. She obviously guessed given that I'd had nothing on when I came out of the bathroom.

Quickly I picked up the hairdryer and scrunch dried my hair. It would look dreadful but at least it would be dry and I could tie it back. The rest could be sorted once I'd got my own things around me. I quickly pulled my hair back into a ponytail and spun around.

"That's it then, shall we go?" Just as I said that, the main door opened and in walked one of the nurses. She watched me as she entered and I quickly remembered what Ben had said on that first day at the Hospital. "Can I help you?" I asked her. Out of the corner of my eye, I saw Anna move, her body shifting from its normal relaxed stance to alert, ready to act. It was as if she had sensed something was about to happen.

"I've been asked to give this to Ms Edwards... you," she said, handing over a folder to Anna containing discharge forms. "But I also need to give you this medication. You must take one tablet twice a day, once with breakfast and once with supper. It is essential that you do not miss a dose," she said. Something about her mannerisms rang alarm bells but before I could say anything Anna had moved and was by my side before I could blink, taking the tablets from the nurse.

"What are these?" she demanded, pulling them out of the blank packaging and inspecting the foil they came in.

"Doc... Doctor Woods left the instruction that **she** was to have them before discharge," the nurse stammered. Anna dived in quickly, not allowing the nurse the chance to say anything.

"Now that **is** strange, you see my Father spoke at length with Dr Woods yesterday evening," she said grabbing the woman's arm and twisting her away from me. "The doctor was adamant that Leah would not need any medication at the point of discharge. He even went as far as to give us his pager details in case Leah needed anything before he visited tomorrow."

Before she could finish, the woman uttered a strange rasping, almost animalistic snarl, sneering maliciously at Anna, before turning back and spitting towards me. Anna flung her arm out across my chest so quickly that I almost didn't register her doing it. She pushed me behind her so that the spittle didn't make contact. With whip like reactions, she then thrust the woman, hard towards the door, protecting me with her body as she did so.

"I suggest you get out of here, RIGHT NOW, before I call for the police. Let me warn you, if either you, **or** your kind, try to make contact with either Leah or my family again we will not be responsible for the results. We will initiate whatever actions we need to take to protect ourselves." The woman snarled at us both, then turned and ran, slamming the door behind her.

Anna turned to me. "Leah, are you ok? There was an angry fire in her eyes, despite her outwardly calm appearance. Unable to speak, I nodded.

She spun on her heels and moved purposefully and rapidly around the room, collecting my personal items as she went. "We need to get out of here, now, Leah, **they** know we are moving you and we don't want any more incidents like that one."

I stared across the bed at her. What on earth did she expect to happen? I was still reeling from the fact that a nurse at this hospital had tried to give me some kind of drug I wasn't supposed to have and had been on the verge of attacking me when she was found out. Slowly I shook my head, trying to get the confused thoughts and images to leave my brain so that I could completely focus on the here and now. As I turned, the corner of my eye caught a quick movement and I registered Anna placing the prescription packet into the bag along with my other meagre belongings.

"Come on then, you must be desperate to get out of here by now," she said, with that beautiful smile on her face. She held the door to the room open for me but I hesitated, I had no idea where I was going, or how we were getting back to their house. Seeing my hesitation she smiled and gently rested a hand on my arm. "It's ok Leah; you will be safe with us. Father will not allow anyone into the house, or grounds, that could harm you, or give you something that you shouldn't have. Our house is one of the oldest in the area – barring your own cottage of course…" she stopped and bit her lip, "Sorry Leah, I didn't mean to bring it up. All of this must be very difficult for you." She stopped talking and we both continued walking along the subtly lit corridor. I walked slightly behind her, observing everything, my mind frantically trying to make sense of what was happening. We turned the corner into a large spacious reception area, decorated more in the style of a boutique hotel than a hospital and before I knew it we were outside, walking towards a sleek silver saloon car. I shivered involuntarily and glanced again at the sky. Angry grey clouds were gathering and the wind was picking up. Yet another storm was coming, I could tell, I just hoped that we would get back to the house before it started.

Anna unlocked the car using the remote and gestured towards the front passenger seat. As I made my way around the car, she cast the bag into the back seat and climbed into the driver's seat, adjusting the seat automatically as she put the key into the ignition. As the engine kicked into a gentle purr, I was startled by an eruption of thunder and again I shivered. Internally I scolded myself – it wasn't as if I was scared of storms and I certainly knew a storm was coming. I glanced across at Anna and caught a look of abstract horror flash across her face. Glancing over at me she caught me looking and instantly her face was once more perfectly composed, she smiled. "Let's get home quickly shall we, before this storm turns really nasty?"

The engine roared and she quickly spun it around, heading for the gates. As she did so a huge fork of lightning shot across the sky, followed almost instantaneously by another clap of thunder. I watched her carefully, trying to control my own concern, as she glanced quickly at the sky, which was beginning to turn a deep shade of purple. Without noticing that I was watching her, she changed down a gear and accelerated, spinning the car off the driveway and onto the B-road. We sped quickly along, in silence.

The storm seemed to worsen with every second. The sky turning darker until you could have mistaken the morning for twilight. With each flash of lightning it appeared as though Anna pushed the car to go faster, until I began to wonder whether we would get stopped by the police.

Before I really had time to think any further, she spun the car around the corner and I realised where we were. Not being a driver myself, I wasn't that familiar with the back roads in and out of our town but now I recognised Borrowell Lane as we sped up towards the town centre. I braced myself, the

Police Station was just around the corner here and we were bound to get stopped.

Before we got to the junction however, she spun the car sharp left, into the driveway alongside the Old School House. I hadn't realised that this is where they lived. Mr Edwards had given me a lovely description of their home but had not actually said where it was. Now I knew and I couldn't help but wonder whether he had withheld that final piece of information deliberately, to prevent us being overheard somehow. Almost as soon as that thought crossed my mind however, I dismissed it. He had said that the family had lived here for a number of years. Therefore it wouldn't be hard for someone to find out where I was. I laughed at myself, "someone" really meant my Dad of course, although I was still struggling to recall the person who had crept into my hospital room that night and now of course there was that horrible nurse too.

The car ground to a halt on the gravel driveway. Anna sprang lightly out of the car and I tailed behind, more slowly. Still apprehensive, I followed her towards the door. Just as we got there she turned.

"Oh, I forgot to say, Mom is the only one home at the moment but I do have a surprise for you – Ben will be home this afternoon."

My heart lurched at the mention of his name but the guarded look in her eyes unnerved me, it was as though she was hiding something, or at least trying to shield me from something. I didn't have time to ask though, as the front door opened wide and out stepped the most beautiful, stylish woman I have ever seen. Approximately three inches taller than her daughter, she had natural wavy blonde hair that was impeccably swept back off her neck. Although dressed in casual clothes, she exuded the same presence and class, which seemed to emanate from the rest of the family. I watched her face carefully. It broke out into the same, open, smile that seemed to bless them all and it appeared to be completely genuine as her eyes, an almost identical shade to her daughters, shone with it.

"Leah, come in, please, I am so pleased to finally meet you my dear. I am Eloise, Joe's wife but please call me by my first name, Mrs Edwards sounds so formal. How are you feeling?" As she spoke she quickly crossed the distance between us and placed her arm across my shoulders. "Anna, bring that small bag will you my darling? Let's get Leah settled quickly, we don't want to tire her out on her first day out of hospital do we?"

With that she steered me inside the beautiful house. Built of brick, the ivy that spread across the front hid the age of the eighteenth century house. The large ornate doorway led into a grand hallway, with a y shaped staircase running off the middle. A black baby grand piano sat to the right of the staircase, I eyed it with interest, wondering if Ben also played that instrument.

As though reading my mind, his mother answered, "The piano is mine, from my younger days, although I don't get so much time to play these days, so I'm a little rusty." Without thinking I responded. "That must be where Ben gets his talent from then," with a smile.

For a split second, the smile on her face froze. "Yes, I suppose it must be, although to be honest I had never thought of it that way. Come on, we'll give you the tour later. You must be tired, so let me show you to your room and you can rest for a while."

Without allowing me time to respond, she swept away in front of me, taking the left hand fork of the staircase and gliding down the landing. Just as it appeared that she couldn't go any further she turned right, through a doorway that I had assumed to be another room and down a small set of seven or eight stairs. I looked around me. Despite the age of the house, the décor was perfect. Decorated with impeccable taste, there were splashes of wine red and terracotta in different rooms, perfectly placed to offset the neutral shades, just like one of the classy boutique hotels that I had seen in magazines. I couldn't see inside the rooms of course but if the public areas were anything to go by, they would be beautiful too.

Mrs Edwards, or "Eloise" as she had told me to call her, stopped suddenly at a door on the left and smiled at me.

"These will be your rooms for as long as you wish to stay with us my dear," she said and with that she opened the door. I looked inside and realised that we had, at some point, entered the old stables, which had been converted to be part of the house at some point in its history. The windows overlooked fields, which I knew would lead to the castle on the right. As I had surmised the room was stunning, painted in a rich luxurious ivory, with splashes of magenta in the bedding and soft furnishings.

"I hope you find it comfortable my dear. Come, Anna, let us leave Leah in peace."

I turned in surprise. I hadn't realised that she had been following us.

She placed my bag on the chair. "We've placed all of your other things in the usual places. The bathroom is through that door on your right. I'll come and find you later if you get lost," she said and with that, Anna and her mother left the room, closing the door behind them.

As they walked away, I could hear them talking and I heard them mention Ben's name. I ran to the door and opened it very slightly, straining to hear what was being said.

"It is too soon for him to come back, particularly with her so close to him. All of those old feelings are going to be rekindled, it just won't be safe for either of them," Anna was saying to her mother.

"Maybe so but it is time. She is Joe's charge, not Ben's, so technically the only thing that he has done wrong is fallen for one of the *special* ones. If the Savant have released him back to us, then they must be content to let nature take its course. All we can do is ensure that she is kept safe and the Harbingers do not get hold of her. If that were to happen it would be the end of everything."

They turned back into the landing of the main house and despite the murmurs, I could no longer make out what they were saying.

I closed the door and absentmindedly walked over to the chest of drawers, delighted to see my own iPod nestled in the docking station there. Selecting one of my playlists, I sat back on the settee and gazed out across the fields, my mind full of the conversation I had just overheard. What did they mean by "charge"? And why was I one of the "special ones"? I resolved to ask someone as soon as the opportunity arose. Finally noticing the view out of the window, I couldn't help wishing that I could actually see the castle from here but I knew it was in the wrong direction. I was glad to see that the weather had begun to clear up at least.

More tired than I realised, I began to doze, for how long I don't know. At some point during the sleep I became aware of raised voices though, both of which I now recognised.

"You are **not** supposed to get involved with her," Joe was saying.

"I appreciate that but how was I supposed to know who she was? You told us nothing about her, only that you had a new charge here in town. How was I to know that she would know nothing of her background? Besides, your charge is nothing to do with me!" Ben yelled back. I stirred with the sound of his voice, even in my sleep I was longing to be with him again.

"That is irrelevant and you know it young man. You know the rules," came the furious reply.

"Sod the rules. I can't help how I feel. Whether it is wrong or not, I have fallen in love with her and you know as well as I do that there is **nothing** that I can do to change that now." The heartbreak in Ben's voice was evident as he spoke and it cut through me like a knife. I couldn't work out why his father was so angry about us but whatever the reason, it was hurting Ben deeply and I didn't want to be responsible for that. I desperately wanted to go and find him, to be held safe in his arms but I had no way of knowing where in the house he was and the last thing I wanted to do was to cause another argument within his family.

I sat there, listening for the sounds of someone coming to get me, allowing me to join them and thought back. I had been so relieved when Joe had invited me to share their home, seeing it as somewhere that I would be safe and believing that I would belong there because of Ben.

If they were so against us being together, then why on earth would they invite me to stay with them, pushing Ben and I closer together against their own wishes? And who on earth were the Savant I had heard Eloise mention?

Secrets

I was back in the wreckage of the car. Dad had somehow managed to get out of the car and was at the door by my side, trying to force it open. I couldn't take my eyes off the lifeless body of my Mother slumped backwards in the driver's seat. Something just didn't look right about the way she was laying, or the injuries that I could see. The windscreen was smashed and the airbag had been deployed and yet I could see the dark, treacle like slither on her face.

A flash of lightning jolted me, I hadn't realised that there was a storm outside. Strange, as Dad didn't look as though he had gotten particularly wet. Momentarily I could see more of my Mother's body, although instantly I wished I hadn't.

A large gaping hole filled her chest, below the upper line of the seatbelt and the thin treacle slither that I could see came from the eye area on the right hand side of her face, which was turned towards me, as though she were about to speak.

I forced myself to look away. How on earth had she been injured so badly? The airbag had deployed, the rags had been visible hanging from the steering wheel. There had been no sign of anything penetrating the car that could have caused that sort of chest injury.

I jumped as the door next to me was wrenched open. A hand reached in and grabbed my arm. For an instant as I looked down, it felt as though the storm lifted me up and carried me away, with the clawed hand still gripping my arm. I could feel the claw, therefore it must be my arm but looking at it, it was the arm of a child.

It was my own scream that woke me up. Disorientated I looked around me at the luxurious surroundings, for a second totally confused about where I was. Although the location was alien, something about the quality and ambience felt familiar and safe, as though I still belonged here despite everything that was flooding back, reminding me of everything that had happened and where I was.

I sat there, in a strange house, surrounded in an illusion of familiar and yet alien furnishings, my body wracked with the sobs and screams of my dreams. No-one to turn to for help and no one I could trust absolutely. The one person who held my heart was somehow being wrenched from me, through no fault of our own and it seemed beyond my control to rescue that situation. The aching emptiness consumed me and it took all my strength to keep the sobs as quiet as I could, not wanting these kind strangers to know what was going on.

The familiar, much loved music threatened to sooth me and in a fit of anguish I threw the docking station remote hard across the room. As soon as it left my hand I regretted it, this was, after all, not my home, nor my belongings to destroy. My normal rubbish aim saved me, this time.

More tired by the events of the last few weeks than I realised, I began to drift away again, lulled by the music, this time into blissful, dream-free sleep.

***

When I awoke, the shadows had grown long and the fields had taken on a gloomy appearance. I lay there for a few moments, absorbing the silence and the beautiful surroundings.

My stomach growled. I had obviously slept through lunch and at this point, had no idea what to do about dinner. I didn't like the idea of mooching around the house looking for food; after all, I was a guest here. But I knew that I was hungry and needed to have something to eat soon. I decided to freshen up, so that at least I would be in a position to accept an invitation to join the family at dinner.

I slowly made my way into the small en-suite, still a little stiff from the accident. Like the rest of the house that I had seen so far, it too was tastefully furnished, in brilliant white with accents of magenta to match the parent room. Finding my own toiletries on the shelf, I clumsily set about cleaning myself up and at least trying to make myself presentable. I didn't hear the door to my room being knocked or opened.

I made my way out of the bathroom, concentrating on tying my hair back off my face, hoping that it would at least look tidy for dinner. I couldn't wait until I was in a position to shower and do my hair properly, without the pain from the accident, or stiffness in my joints from lack of use.

Lost in thought I didn't even notice him at first. As I turned from the dressing table his wonderful face smiled slowly and hesitantly at me, as though unsure of what my reaction would be. I couldn't fight the urge. I flung myself across the room at him, hugging him as tightly as I possibly could.

"Leah, it's ok, let go… you're safe here," he murmured into my hair, gently unwrapping my fingers and arms from around him and stepping back, away from my kiss.

I pulled back, hurt. What was the problem? Although I really knew the answer to that, I didn't want to accept that he was giving in, trying to stop any relationship now, before it became too late.

He held both of my hands in his, refusing to bring his eyes to meet mine.

"Ben, what is it, what is the matter?" I asked, pain evident in my voice.

"Leah, it isn't you, I just think things were starting to go too fast. Liberation has the regional finals next weekend and I really need to focus on my music and get ready for University right now." He stepped back further, almost tripping over the little coffee table behind him. "I only came to say hello and to invite you to come and join us for dinner."

As the last sentence left his mouth he turned and made his way to the door, appearing to be more comfortable now that he had put some distance between us.

Totally confused and more than a little hurt, I followed meekly, not capable of arguing for fear of bursting into tears and giving away the depth of my own feelings.

I must have appeared very unsociable during dinner, I spoke only when spoken to and ate little, considering how hungry I had been less than thirty minutes earlier. The family spoke fondly and calmly to one another, with the odd sideways comment between them, as they attempted to lighten the mood. I caught both Eloise and Anna watching me carefully at various times, although they were very adept at masking being caught. There was none of the light hearted chatter that I had experienced at Jen's house between her and her siblings. Perhaps this was normal and they were the unique family?

I couldn't wait to get away from the table and I could hear Mom's voice reprimanding me for my poor manners. Although somewhat shy, I had always been able to hold a conversation when required to. This was different though. Although still astonishingly tired from the accident and... withdrawal I suppose you would call it, at this precise moment in time I felt as though my heart had been ripped right out of my body and was being held, still beating, by the person sitting next to me at the table.

As soon as was just decent, I excused myself from the table, left the dining room and practically ran to my room. I could hear the argument starting as soon as I left the room.

"Why did you go to her room?" Joe demanded.

"She didn't come down for lunch and it was obvious that **no-one** had been up to invite her, so I was concerned that she didn't miss two meals in one day. She is still very weak." Ben replied.

"How long were you with her – what contact did you have?" Came the accusatory reply.

"I was there for a matter of minutes and we barely even spoke," he almost spat back. "Besides, I've told you, she is not **my** charge, so I really don't see the problem here. I know she isn't one of **us** but she **is** one of the special ones. Falling in love is not a crime, as you two well know."

I would have loved to have hung around, just to hear the rest of that particular conversation. My bruised heart lurched at the mention of love, however the dining room door smashed open and I stifled a shriek. I hurried back to my room, as quickly as I could manage.

Seconds later the door to my room flew open and Ben tore in. Before I could speak, or do anything, he scooped me up and held me close. "I'm sorry," he said, "I just can't do this." My heart began to flutter as I fought to form any words but before I could speak, he continued. "They keep telling me that we are not allowed to be together, because we are so different but I cannot help how I feel and neither do I want to change it."

We stood together, as close as we could get, hearts and breaths synchronised, heads resting together. The tension was real; I could feel it in Ben's shoulders and the way he held me. It was as if he was afraid to let go, afraid of just where it might lead. I longed for him to talk to me, to explain what the problem was. I was certain that *this* could not be wrong – how could something that felt this right be anything but meant to be?

The door to my room flew open. "Ben, your Father is coming; you'd best leave by the other door." I heard Eloise say. I stepped slightly away, desperate to not let go but also conscious that I was a guest in this house and I did not want to cause any further problems for my hosts.

Ben groaned. "But…"

"Don't be silly now, it is easy for me to see how much you mean to one another but your Father needs convincing that *they* will be ok with it. As yet we have no response to our request for an audience, you know that. Ben, don't provoke a situation that is beyond repair, leave now and let me deal with your Father and Leah."

He looked at me and the pain in his eyes sliced through me like a knife. I knew that I had to act, that if I didn't the situation would deteriorate into unthinkable circumstances. Gently I pushed him away.

"Go, Ben, now. We can get through this together and work things out. You don't need to create problems with your own Father right now." I heard footsteps marching up the hallway and the tone of my voice changed. "How does he get out? Please help us," I begged Eloise.

Wordlessly, she strode around the bed and across to the little bookshelf, by its side sat a very old, wrought iron dog, that looked about as old as the house itself. Reaching down she gently felt behind its ear, as though she were tickling it. Smoothly and silently a doorway opened in the perfectly matched wallpaper.

"Quickly, go now, I will answer any questions that you may have later," she urged.

Squeezing my hand tightly, Ben hurried over and stepped through the doorway. As soon as he was clear, Eloise tickled the dog's nose and the doorway disappeared, just as Joe appeared in the doorway. He glared around the room and the surprise only registered for a few seconds.

"Eloise, here you are, I wondered where you had gone off to," he said, eyes still darting around the room.

"I just wanted to check on our guest dear, she was so quiet at dinner. And I am responsible for her while she is under our roof, so I wanted to check that everything was ok." She smiled at us both. "Leah, if you need anything while you are here, a drink, or if you are hungry, please feel free to help yourself to anything in the kitchen. I keep bottled water here in the bedside cabinet for guests and there are glasses in the other side too."

She went to walk around the bed to show me but Joe was there first.

"I'll get it Eloise," he said, trying and failing, to subtly look inside the en-suite while he was round there. Realising that we had seen him, he offered, "I just wanted to be sure we had left some towels in there for you."

Eloise muttered something under her breath and shook her head. The slightest tinge of pink flashed across Joe's cheeks. I watched them both carefully, Eloise showed absolutely no outward sign, as far as I could tell, of what had just happened but why had she protected us like that?

She strode across the room and linked her arm through Joe's. "Come on darling, let's leave Leah alone, she has had more than enough to contend with recently and needs to be able to settle and make herself feel at home. She's not likely to do that with us two oldies hanging over her is she?" With that she started to leave, steering him skilfully out of the room. As they turned the corner, she glance back at me, winked and nodded towards the bookcase. She closed the door behind them as they left.

For several minutes I stood there, unable to make sense of what had just happened. None of it seemed to fit, the arguments, Eloise's assistance, anything. Coming to my senses, I thought of Ben and following Eloise's direction, I returned to the bookcase and tickled the dogs' ear. Nothing happened. Confused I looked down and realised that I had not gone to the back of the ear. As I did, I felt a little switch, pressed it and the door glided open again.

To my surprise Ben was standing there. Confused I pulled him out and peered through the doorway. Sure enough, there was a long gloomy corridor, lit entirely by what appeared to be natural light coming through from the end. I couldn't help wondering where it went.

However, as I made to go in and investigate, I felt Ben hold me back. I withdrew back into my room and looked at him questioningly.

"Don't Leah, it would be too easy to get caught and I don't want to have to go away again," he said.

"Ben, please, tell me what is going on. Why would you have to go away again and what on earth is wrong with us falling in love like…." I stopped as a look of pain shot across his face.

"Please don't Leah, we can't. I **do** love you, I hope you know that but it just isn't possible for us to be together. If they found out…"

"But, Eloise has just helped us, stopped Joe from finding out you were here, so she must understand, even just a little." I interrupted, desperate to make him see sense.

He shook his head slowly. "I'm not talking about them," he responded, then he stopped, as though he could not go any further. With a deep sigh he reached out and pulled me to him. "I can't really understand why this is so wrong either Leah but we do have to be careful and not show how deeply we feel for one another. Right now it isn't safe to even think about it. Please, let's just spend a little time together for now, while we can."

At that he pulled away slightly and took me by the hand. Leading me to the sofa, he sat down, almost pulling me down so that I lay against his side. He wrapped his arms around me, holding me tight and kissing the side of my head softly.

"How can this be so wrong?" he whispered.

I turned to him, trying to understand the pained expression on his face. He refused to meet my gaze so I simply leant forward and kissed him very gently on the side of his face. At my touch, a soft whimper escaped and he pulled me towards me, smothering my face and lips with kisses of his own. I couldn't help but respond. For a few minutes we were lost in one another's kissed, as though some kind of starvation had set in. Then, suddenly he thrust me away from him, almost pushing me off the sofa in the process.

"Leah, we can't. If we give in to our feelings now, they will take me away from you forever and I couldn't stand that. If we resist our feelings and remain strong, at least I will be able to stay here, with **them**. At least that would mean that I can be with you and look after you at least, even if I can't be *with* you in the way I want to be." He hung his head and there was an almost desperate appearance about the way he sat. I watched him, full of nerves. What was going on? I didn't want to be parted from him either but I wasn't sure that I was strong enough to be with him and not give in to these feelings.

With a deep sigh, he extricated himself from the sofa and stood up. He held onto my hand as he walked away, giving it one final gentle squeeze before finally letting go. He stroked the dog's nose as he stepped through the doorway, which we had left open and before I could stop him the doorway glided closed and he was gone.

I ran to the door, holding back the tears that threatened to blind me. Pressing the button in the dogs ear, I waited impatiently for the door to open wide enough for me to fit through, it seemed to take so much longer this time. Slipping through, I went to close the door and then quickly thought better of it. As it stood I had no idea where the passage led to and needed to be sure I could get back to my room.

I hurried towards the end of the passage, certain that I would find Ben waiting. Built of the same stone as the house and stables, cobwebs and dust lined the passage, suddenly making me feel very uneasy. It went on much further than it had first appeared to from the door in my room and just as I approached the end, I found it turned off quite sharply to the right. Puzzled I slowed slightly, I needed to be careful now, as this meant that it wound back into the main building of the house and I wasn't quite sure where I would eventually end up.

I turned the corner and came to an abrupt stop. In front of me was a huge glass window, facing out into a lovely little courtyard. There was still so much about this place that I didn't know, I hadn't even realised that the buildings would create such a courtyard from the variety of extensions that had taken place over the years.

Abruptly I started to scurry backwards. On the other side of the window, standing in the speckled sunlight, stood Joe and Anna, talking in great depth about something. Anna lifted her hand up and placed it against the glass as she was talking, glancing slightly towards me as she did so. I froze, desperately hoping that I was far enough back for her not to notice me. Mesmerised by the interaction between father and daughter I leant against the wall, anxious not to be spotted but also entranced by what was playing out before me. They were talking animatedly, hands adding emphasis to the words that I was unable to hear.

I jumped as Ben appeared just slightly out of their field of vision, coming from behind slight protrusion in the brickwork. Panicked I stood there helplessly, wondering how they would react when they saw him appear and whether he would be quick enough to register their presence first and so be able to not give away the location of the passage. I breathed again when I saw him hesitate slightly, take a deep breath and then quickly alter the line he was walking from, so as to appear to be coming from another place entirely.

I saw him smile and call out – although I couldn't quite hear what was actually said, as the sounds were muffled by the glass.

I watched the family unit with interest. Anna was talking very animatedly to her father, gesturing openly towards Ben from time to time and although he had more of his back to me, I could see that Joe's response was just as animated. Ben stood there, listening to the conversation, his sadness written all over his face. The conversation obviously changed direction, as he suddenly became very animated too. Whatever it was that Joe had said, Ben responded quickly and his frustration and anger were both evident in his actions. Anna joined in and from where I stood, only being able to judge the conversation by their body language; it appeared that she was also agreeing with Ben. The volume started to increase between the three participants, although I still couldn't work out what was being said, until Ben shouted:

"I don't care about that, you can take it all away from me if you must, Leah is **not** my charge and I had absolutely no idea who she was when we met. We have done **nothing** wrong. I **want** to be with her – what can be so wrong with that?"

With that he turned and stormed out of the little courtyard. I heard Joe shout, "Ben but..." and then Ben was out of sight. I couldn't tear myself away from the little scene in front of me, as Joe's shoulders slumped. Anna put her arm around his shoulders and leant her head on him. Suddenly I was swamped with memories of similar times with my own Father. Unable to control the swell of emotion, I turned and ran back up the passageway to my room.

I closed the door as I had seen Eloise do, then threw myself on the bed, drowning with emotion and the sense of loss. I buried my head in the pillows and sobbed, unable to control the flow or the feelings.

Agreement

I was back at the Castle, running towards Leicester's Gatehouse , the sound of the little girl crying always seemed to be right on top of me but no matter which way I went, or where I ran, I couldn't seem to find her.

I ran towards the car park, desperate to be able to help her, she must be absolutely petrified by now. The roar was getting louder too, although it wasn't managing to drown out the girl's crying.

The sweet smell of damp grass after a dry spell hit me as I ran. I hadn't noticed it start to rain; I was too preoccupied in finding the child. As I reached the road, the smell was stronger. Suddenly a man grabbed me but before I could resist or scream, that same safe, comfortable feeling hit and I knew instantly who it was. I struggled to pull away slightly, why couldn't he hear the little girl and help me find her?

I heard the car approaching, I think I was almost waiting for it this time. Without being asked I jumped towards the open door, the man following very closely behind me. Once inside I glanced instinctively towards the front passenger seat, there was no-one sitting there this time, so where was my Dad?

The car accelerated away before I could begin to ask any questions. I struggled to put the seatbelt on, annoyed with myself, it wasn't normally this difficult a task. As I went to attach it I looked down, still frustrated at my struggles. I realised firstly how wet my clothes were, clinging to my body in places but something was wrong, what was I wearing? These were not the clothes I had been wearing. These were the clothes of a little girl, not any little girl but me, from when I was about nine, one of my favourite outfits of that time, with sparkly trimmings on the jeans.

Puzzled I glanced down at my hands, still fumbling with the seatbelt, just as the man next to me gently took it off me to secure it probably. They were the hands of a little girl.

Now I was completely confused. In desperation I looked towards the driver, seeking an explanation

or at least some understanding of what was going on.
My mother's eyes looked back at me through the rear
view mirror.

I woke up more gradually than usual after one
of those dreams, whether it was exhaustion from the
emotion of earlier I don't know but I lay there facing
the wall for a short while, my mind blankly searching
for an explanation. It just didn't make any sense to
me at all. Why should they return to the Castle now,
after the more recent dreams had been focussed more
on the accident? Not that that made much sense
either, because I hadn't been in the car the night
Mom had died.

After a while my shoulder started to ache from
the position I had been lying in, so reluctantly I flung
my legs over the side of the bed and sat up. Out of
the corner of my eye I caught something. When I
turned and looked, sitting serenely on my sofa was
Eloise, her hands folded gently in her lap and eyes
cast towards the floor.

At my movement she looked up and smiled
gently. The look in her eyes told me that she

understood more about my emotions and perhaps even my dreams, than I wanted her to right now. The reassuring smile started in her eyes first and then spread to her mouth, as though she also understood that thought too. Despite her assistance earlier with Ben, I still found her unsettling, she seemed so perfect all of the time. It was as though she understood your thoughts too. I watched her warily.

"Leah, I know you've been going through your own personal kind of hell recently and I know that you have very deep feelings for my son too," she shook her head gently as I started to interrupt, "from what I can see, he has grown just as fond of you. It may not seem like it to you right now but you are both very young and in reality you know very little about one another. Ben has a very important role to play in the world as he gets older and, as his parents, his guides, we are just concerned that this current… infatuation… may disrupt that. Now personally I am of the opinion that we must let this matter run its course – if we try to interfere, or prevent you being together we are more likely to drive you towards one another. Joe, on the other hand, strongly believes that we should forcibly keep you apart. Having said all of that, we have a duty to ensure that you recover fully from recent events and are also kept safe, so therefore you will be both, for a while, be living under our roof. I therefore want to ask you to make me a promise."

She paused, watching me carefully, " a promise, that, if I permit you to spend time together and you to go to the finals at the weekend, that you will respect our concerns and ensure that this relationship does not... develop any further while you are under our roof? In return I will speak to Joe and ensure that he goes easier on Ben for a while, to allow him to focus on his music and the upcoming finals." She finally stopped, eyebrows raised with the question, waiting for an answer. My mind now racing, I took a deep breath, as I searched for the right words in my answer.

"Eloise, I appreciate your concern and I admit that I have very strong, powerful, feelings for Ben. However, I am not quite sure what you are asking here. We are, after all, just two young people that have met and become close, developing feelings for one another, that is all. Nothing that could be considered in any way inappropriate has happened between us, if that **is** what you are trying to suggest. Quite frankly, if it is, I am a little offended by the implication that you think it would at this point in time. I am eternally grateful to you both for giving me this refuge when I needed it most but as for my… feelings for Ben, neither of us could say right now where our relationship is going, if in fact it is going anywhere. All we do know right now is how we feel about one another; it is far too early to have considered anything else."

I took a deep breath, trying to calm the shaking inside. "If you want me to leave then I will, after all it is your home. Having said all of that, of course I want to be able to spend time with Ben and be there to support him in the finals but I am a guest here, so the decision must lie with you. I will **not** however lie to him, or you, about how I feel and my need to be with him. Which is not just because of our, my, feelings but also that he is the only person in this world right now that understands a little about what is going on in my life." I stopped for breath, my insides shaking uncontrollably, my mind now numb with panic. What would I do if they asked me to leave and even worse, prevented me from ever seeing Ben again? I had nowhere to go and suddenly I felt very vulnerable and childlike, just like the little girl in my dreams.

For a brief second I thought I saw Eloise's eyes widen slightly and then she smiled softly. "Leah, we have no intention of asking you to leave. We have to protect you and ensure that you are kept safe. All that I ask is that you respect our concerns for our son and if you agree to do that and abide by what I have asked, then no more needs to be said. I shall deal with Joe about any other issues – is that okay with you? Do I have your word?"

I nodded, relieved, yet still numb. "Of course you do and thank you," I whispered. With that Eloise smiled and walked towards me, wrapping me in her arms.

"Thank you that is all I ask," she said, squeezing me gently. Almost floating, she left the room quickly and silently.

I stood there uncertain what to do after that. The last thing that I felt like doing was going downstairs and being sociable, despite the ache inside me, gnawing at me, constantly reminding me of my need to see Ben.

Eventually, I have no idea how long after Eloise had left, I walked into the sitting area of the room. Somehow I felt the need to avoid where she had just sat, so I sat on the chaise longue, aching for the last time that I had sat on a similar piece of furniture. For lack of any other form of distraction, I reached for the remote and turned the little television on. Flicking through the channels I found an old episode of Bones running and settled back to watch, glad to have something to take my mind away from what had happened.

Rehearsal

The episode of Bones had long finished, followed by an equally old CSI, when the door to my room swung gently open. In strode Ben, full of smiles, carrying a tray with two mugs of hot chocolate and a few biscuits.

"Thought you might be peckish," he said, still smiling, although now it appeared to be more than a little forced.

I sat up warily, memories of the conversation with Eloise still stinging my mind. Looking less certain of himself he sat on the edge of the same seat that she had occupied a couple of hours earlier. Keen to avoid my gaze, he busied himself taking the mugs off the tray and placing them on the little table, followed by the plate of biscuits. Eventually though he looked up.

"I'm sorry," he said simply, "I know I behaved badly. I just wish I could explain it all to you but it is just so complicated. Mother told me that she had spoken to Father and of course you, so it is ok now – we don't have to keep secrets anymore."

I watched him carefully; surely he knew the detail of what Eloise had said to me, how could he be so blasé about it?

"Do you know what was said?" I blurted out, immediately annoyed with myself for not wording it more carefully.

He flushed slightly. "Yes, she did tell me and I wish she had spoken to me first, because I could have put their minds at rest rather than upset you like this."

"What do you mean?" I butted in.

"Leah, you have to realise that my parents have old fashioned ideas and that some of the ideas out there about the way young people behave now causes them some considerable concern. They had seen the change in me recently and when they realised the cause, they jumped to the wrong conclusions. Please don't be upset, I've put them straight and I'm sorry that you had to go through that."

He looked at me almost pleadingly. Despite the still recent wounds, I couldn't resist that look and I smiled. Taking that as encouragement, he grabbed a biscuit and shuffled back on the seat.

Too shell shocked to discuss anything right now, I stood, retrieved one for myself and went and sat on the chair alongside. Desperate as I was to feel his arms around me again, the last thing I wanted was to be found like that.

My choice of seat and the obvious reason behind it did not go unnoticed and his face fell.

"Leah, please don't be like this..." but almost as he spoke a brisk knock came at the door and it opened almost simultaneously. Joe stood there and in the instant it took him to register where we were and how we were seated, the look on his face flashed from concern to relief.

"I was just checking that you'd brought Leah a drink, Ben. It's getting late, so don't keep her awake for too long now, she still needs her rest to fully recuperate." He hesitated slightly, awaiting some kind of response. Ben looked back at his Father and gave an almost imperceptible nod, satisfied with that

Joe walked away. I had the sneaking suspicion that leaving the door open was not an accident.

Ben noticed it too and went to stand to go and close it again. Without thinking my hand shot out to stop him. As it made contact a shock ran up my arm and I instinctively pulled away. The look on his face said it all, the pain and sadness of the perceived rejection.

"Ben, please, don't be like that. You know how I feel about you but you also know what your parents think. I would be surprised if you didn't know exactly what Eloise has said to me. I do not want to disrespect their wishes, or give them any further cause for concern but it doesn't alter my feelings for you." I tried to look away but Ben grabbed my arm and pulled me up to him. My heart began to race at being so close to him again; my nostrils filled with his warm musky scent as he slowly and gently lifted my chin to gaze into my eyes, then he lowered his head and kissed me. Unable to control my own need, I couldn't stop my response to him. My free hand found its way up to his neck, tangling in his hair as the heat started to build. Despite the longing inside me, I finally managed to regain control and pull away.

"We shouldn't," I said, my breath catching in my throat as my body ached to be close to him again.

"We are not doing anything wrong Leah, nor are we breaking their rules. I'm not trying to push things any further."

I shook my head, praying that Ben couldn't see just how much effort it took for me to resist being this close to him.

"Tomorrow is the dress rehearsal and Saturday is the final," I stated. "You need your rest and to keep everything calm, so you can focus on winning."

With that I reluctantly extracted myself from his arms and walked to the door. "Come on, it's time we both went to sleep." Dejectedly he walked slowly after me but I was unable to stop myself reaching for his arm as he got to the door.

"Ben, I've fallen for you pretty hard but I don't want to go against my promise to Eloise. That doesn't mean that I don't want to be with you, just that we need to be careful and take our time."

He leaned forward and kissed me very gently and then left the room, letting go of my hand at the last possible moment.

I stood there for quite a while, staring after him, trying to restore balance in my head. Eventually I closed the door, pottered around the room getting changed and went to bed.

I lay there in the large comfortable bed, mind full of wandering thoughts and ideas. For the first time in quite a while there was no storm outside and as I started to dose off, there were none of the usual indications of one of those dreams coming.

It was still dark when I awoke but I could sense that I was no longer alone. Still disorientated by the strange surroundings, I lay there for a while, afraid of turning to see who, or what, was with me.

Finally, mind now wide-awake, I gave in and rolled over to face the room. My eyes sought out the unusual as they also grew accustomed to the changing shadows in the room. Eventually they focussed on the chair and I made out a man's shape. Heart beginning to race, I gathered the covers around me, wondering whether I could make it to the little en-suite quickly and lock myself away. The secret passageway was just too close to where he sat, I couldn't be sure of closing the door before he followed.

My heart started to slow very slightly as I made out the shape, at least it wasn't one of those Harbingers from my dreams. As my eyes focussed, my brain finally recognised the figure. It was Joe.

Realising I was awake, he rose very quietly and disappeared through the partially open door, without saying a word.

When I awoke the following morning, I was convinced that it had been a dream. It wasn't as if I hadn't had bizarre dreams in the past and there had been times that they had even seemed to come to life during the haze of waking. Besides, why on earth would he just be sitting there and watching me? That would just be too weird.

I glanced at the clock on the television; it was almost nine thirty! Jumping out of bed, I had to resort to grabbing the wall quickly due to the dizziness it brought on. Waking at this time was almost unheard of for me. Ever since the nightmares had got worse, I had become an early riser.

I tried to rush about the room with hilarious consequences. Despite showing daily improvement, my ease of movement was still hampered from the injuries incurred during the accident; therefore simple tasks such as showering dressing and even making myself as presentable as I could were clumsy to say the least. The dress rehearsals started at twelve and I was ravenous, so I needed to get some breakfast first.

Once ready I dashed out into the hallway and almost collided with Anna in the process. She flushed slightly with surprise and then linked her arm through mine as she turned to face the same way.

"I was just coming to check on you," she said. "I wanted to be sure you didn't miss breakfast, as I guess you'll be at the Hall all afternoon?" she queried, I glanced nervously at her face, trying to gauge what was meant by the comment. There was nothing to indicate that it was a trick question, so I nodded slowly.

"As long as no-one has a problem with me going, then yes, I would like to be there." I admitted, still watching her closely.

"That's great, I was hoping you would say that," she responded a huge grin on her face. "It gives me an excuse to come too, without being the only girl there and giving my brother reason to rib me yet again about Rich."

She caught me watching her and blushed. "Yes, ok, so I like him a little, there's no harm in that is there? He's only just over three years older than me," she added. I stopped and looked at her in surprise.

"But I thought he was the same age as Ben?" I queried, trying to picture him in my head as I said it. There couldn't be that much between them, surely. I visualised him, about six foot three with reddish brown hair. He was slightly broader than both Will and Ben, as though he had filled out more than they had, so I suppose he could have been around a year older.

"There's not even a year between them, Ben is not quite two and a half years older than me, which would make him eighteen months older than you." She grinned at my surprise. "I guess you assumed he was the same age?"

I nodded. Why should it bother me that he wasn't – after all, a year and a half was hardly a generation was it? I did feel bad though for arguing about it with Dad though, as he had obviously gauged correctly that there was an age difference between us. I shivered slightly at the memory of that night and Anna squeezed my arm closer to her.

"Come on, you must be ravenous," she said and practically pulled me towards the kitchen with her enthusiasm.

We could hear them talking before we got to the kitchen and the smell of warm toast and cooking bacon wafted down the corridor, making my stomach growl with anticipation. As we entered the room, Rich was sitting on the work surface, laughing at the punch line to a joke Will had just told. He glanced over towards us as we entered and his look lingered for a second too long on Anna, before he turned and acknowledged me too. Then, jumping down, he gestured to Will, grabbing a couple of cool bags as he left through the back door. Will grabbed the remaining bags and then followed him back to the car.

I smiled quietly as I busied myself getting my breakfast, despite not really knowing the band that well it seemed obvious to me that he was, at least in some part, aware of her feelings for him. For some reason that knowledge made me smile, despite desperately trying to avoid Ben's eyes, which I could feel following me as he waited for some kind of acknowledgment. Despite the events of the previous evening, I was still really cautious about showing our affection in front of his family.

When we arrived, Symphony Hall was alive with people. Throughout the day the numbers rose and fell, depending I suppose on what was happening at the time. Despite there being no formal audience, it was obvious that many friends and family had arrived to help their own band prepare and boost their confidence; the others must have simply been onlookers or media taking a sneak peak. The noise inside the hall itself was tremendous as people tried to rehearse and test last minute ideas in the background, then silence would be called while each finalist was put through their gruelling paces, to check sound and light arrangements and ensure that they knew exactly how to work the stage on the following night.

The whole day passed in a whirl, despite my initial reservations, Anna turned out to be fantastic company. I really couldn't help but like her. Her knowledge of music, singing along with the tracks that we knew in between the formal rehearsals, dancing in the auditorium and even just messing around, – it all made me really excited for the following night and the finals. Everyone that was there seemed to be on a high and they were really friendly towards one another. This seemed a little strange to me for such a high profile competition –

you would normally expect maybe a little antagonism as a result of the competitiveness. I did get the strange sensation of being watched sometimes, probably because we were so vocal in support of Liberation but I didn't care. For once and in what seemed like a lifetime, I was happy and having fun. Even the storm that had erupted just after we left the house couldn't dampen our spirits.

When we got back to the house it was very late. Eloise had stopped to collect fish and chips on the way home and we all sat around, along with Rich and Will, eating our supper and talking into the early hours. Ben had perched on the arm of my chair, as close as he could get, for most of the evening and no-one had batted an eyelid. Anna was desperately flirting with Rich but he was obviously not interested, even I could see that and I felt sorry for her. Eventually it was time to go to bed – Rich and Will left and we all dragged ourselves away. I clambered into the comfortable welcoming bed and fell straight asleep, my dreams filled with happy thoughts and memories for once.

The Finals

The sun, where it could escape from behind the curtains, cast patterns across the room when I awoke. I lay there for a few moments, feeling rested and calm. I'd had the best night sleep that I could remember for quite a while and I basked in the luxurious feeling.

Finally and more than a little reluctantly, I registered the light coming through the curtains and realised it was already well into the morning. I clambered out of bed and rushed as quickly as my injuries would allow around my room, sorting out clothes to wear for the finals and thinking through the other acts that I'd seen rehearsing the day before – they were all really good and much as every inch of me wanted to believe that Liberation would win, there were a few acts that I really could see coming in the final three. I found myself offering up a prayer as I continued to get ready, asking that the band would do well.

As I opened the door to my room, the smell of the cooking breakfast wafted in and my stomach growled in response, sending me hurrying towards the kitchen in hungry anticipation. As I entered the room, my heart lurched at the sight of Ben sitting at the table, the sunlight catching his movements as he ate. He looked up at smiled and my stomach flipped over in response. Suddenly very flustered, I averted my eyes and busied myself gathering the food I wanted for breakfast. I wasn't saved for long though, as the only remaining seat at the table was directly opposite him.

Eventually I had to look up and found that he was watching me, a soft smile on his face. Embarrassed, I quickly glanced around – Anna, Joe and Eloise were all busy discussing the day ahead and seemed oblivious to what we were doing. A little reassured, I smiled back, to be greeted with an even wider grin.

"Good morning," he said quietly. "How did you sleep?"

"Very well thank you, no bad dreams last night for a change," I responded – did I imagine it, or did I see Joe react slightly to my last comment? I really couldn't tell, it was probably just my imagination in overdrive again.

I focussed on eating – by the state of their plates, the others had all been down a good while before me and I knew Will and Rich were due any moment. Just as the thought crossed my mind, I heard the front door open and in they walked. Anna's face lit up at the sight of Rich and she shifted her position so that he could better see her. As usual, he seemed completely oblivious to her advances and they both helped themselves to coffee.

The volume of conversation in the room rose as the three members agreed on any minor changes that were needed for the final. Anna seemed undeterred and kept her bright gaze on Rich, captivated by his every word. Will, who I now knew wrote most of the music, led most of the discussion. I felt much more secure in watching Ben in this environment, enjoying seeing him so animated and involved but comfortable in that no-one could find fault in this.

Eloise looked at the clock. "Right, it is time we were off. There's still the final set up to do before tonight. Ben, are you going to take your car too, so that you guys can clear away at the end?" she asked. Ben nodded his response.

I stood to go with Eloise, Joe and Anna. As I made my way between the table and the counter where he was now perched, Ben lightly grabbed my hand. I felt my heart thud at his touch and I glanced at him quickly.

"I'll go with your parents – leave you three to finalise your plans," I said, smiling as realistically as I could.

Ben's face fell slightly. "There's room for you in my car if you'd prefer?" he said. What was he saying? Of course I would prefer to be with him, couldn't he tell that simply from my reactions?

Despite these thoughts running through my mind, I shook my head. "No, it's best if you three concentrate on the finals for now – I promise to drive home with you when you win." At that I gently removed my hand from his grasp and hurriedly followed Anna, who was the last one disappearing out of the door.

She threw me a strange glance as I climbed into the car beside her.

"I thought you'd be travelling with Ben?" she murmured, "I know I would have given half a chance." I struggled to smother a smile – she was infatuated.

"No, I thought it best to let them focus on what they've got to achieve tonight. The last thing I want to be is a distraction for Ben," I replied. In the front passenger seat Joe nodded, as though satisfied with my response. I strapped myself in as the car sped off – what was it about this family and the speed they drove their cars I wondered to myself; it was obviously a family trait. The car quickly wound its way through the roads, passed the castle and onward towards the city centre. The sky turned more and more purple as we drove and I shivered, anticipating yet another storm ahead. Joe turned slightly at my movement.

"Are you warm enough Leah? There's a blanket in the boot, we can stop and get it for you if you need it?" he asked, his smile evident in his voice.

Eloise's hands tightened on the steering wheel as he spoke. "Or would you prefer I turn the heat up?"

"No, please, I'm fine, it just looks as though there is another storm coming, that's all. I can't remember the last time we had quite so many storms this close together." I answered, anxious not to be any kind of burden. A quick glance passed between driver and passenger. I couldn't help wondering whether I would ever completely understand this family.

We sped through the streets, which were surprisingly quiet even for quite early on a Saturday morning. Eloise had been right, it was better to leave when we did rather than risk getting caught up in the shopping traffic. It wasn't long before we were pulling into the nearest car park. Another bonus, we managed to park on the level that had the walkway straight across to Symphony Hall. Before long we had carried the instruments and equipment across the walkway and into the hall.

The next couple of hours were spent rehearsing and moving the apparatus, until the stage was laid out with all the equipment that the individual groups had bought. I was amazed that the stage manager had managed to achieve it all, while still allowing enough space on stage for the bands to perform.

The time flew and before I knew it, the final rehearsal and instructions had been given. My stomach was churning with nerves, so I couldn't begin to imagine what the performers were feeling. Although they were doing their best to hide it, all of the bands were showing signs of nerves – Will was constantly checking the tuning on his guitar while Rich was pacing up and down the little space we occupied, fingers practicing notes in the air. Ben was quiet and focussed, deep in thought but I could see the tiny crease above his nose as he concentrated, maybe just a little too hard. Every bone in me wanted to reach over and smooth that crease, help ease his nerves just a little but I knew it probably wouldn't help.

As I was watching him he suddenly caught my eye. In a move almost indiscernible to anyone else, he gestured for me to follow him, then stood and walked away. Despite my reservations, after a few moments, I followed.

I sped up as I reached the corner, I didn't want to lose sight of him and for him then to think that I hadn't followed as he has asked. As I rounded the bend, a hand grabbed me and before I could respond, his mouth crushed mine, forcing a willing response as he turned me into an alcove away from prying eyes. His lips and tongue sought out mine and I yielded readily. Seconds passed as the world began to spin again and I would have fallen if it hadn't been for Ben's arms. A surreptitious cough interrupted us and I felt a different heat rise to my cheeks.

Ben turned, shielding me from the onlooker's sight, then he relaxed and laughed. Anna's voice broke the silence,

"Come on you two, otherwise you will be missed and you don't want to spoil anything now do you?" she grinned. Indicating with her hand for Ben to go first, she linked her arm through mine. "We're just going to hang back together for a second, so that they see us walking back and think you've been with me." Again I was struck by the innate calm that this family were all able to exhibit.

As we walked back towards the auditorium, the change in the atmosphere struck me. More people had started to arrive, to cheer their favourite band or region on and the excitement was building. I stopped to pick up one of the programmes and review the running order, even though I knew it by heart:

Region	Band	Genre
Walsall	Prophets	Folk
Stafford	Beginnings	Acoustic
Worcester	Moments	Motown
Solihull	Risen	Pop
West Bromwich	Freedom	Metal
Birmingham	Reflection	Soul
Warwick	Liberation	Rock

None of the contestants were quite sure how the final running order had been decided upon. It didn't fit alphabetically or by size of the region. Whatever the reason, it worked, or seemed to during the dress rehearsal. "Prophets" got the spirit moving with their folk music and by the time we reached "Moments", the audience had just wanted to dance. The beautiful soul of "Your Reflection" quietened the mood a little before we ended with the passion from "Liberation." Ben had been delighted to go last but I wasn't so sure. The others all had the chance to set the bar and it would make it very difficult for them. They seemed to manage it in the earlier rehearsals though, or was that my bias talking?

In the short time it had taken me to review the programme, the auditorium had almost completely filled up and I rushed over to where the family sat. Although too far away from Ben for my liking, the view from these side areas were fantastic and at least I had a backstage pass for the end of the show, even if I did only qualify for it as I was lined up to help them clear away.

The atmosphere was building by the second but above the murmured conversations and rustle of papers and coats, I heard the storm outside and shivered. Eloise turned to me in concern and I smiled and shook my head. I wasn't cold but these perpetual storms were really getting to me now.

As the lights started to dim, I caught sight of Ben out of the corner of my eye and gave him my biggest brightest smile, hoping it conveyed my absolute faith in him. As I did, I caught a movement out of the corner of my eye but when I focussed, it had gone. I didn't have time to think about it anymore, as the lights focussed on the stage and the compere, a local celebrity and comedian, walked on stage. The audience erupted in welcome, the excitement evident. Before long the competition started in earnest.

By the time we got to the interval, I was glad that I wasn't on the panel of judges. They'd sat there, watching each performance and making notes, sometimes tapping a pen or moving their shoulders in time with the music but otherwise giving very little away. I'd thought the dress rehearsal had been good but so far, each of the bands had managed to improve on that performance – they must have been nervous but to me it didn't show.

I started to feel really uncomfortable. The storm was raging fiercely outside and every so often, when the lights weren't picking out a performer, the darkness inside was shot through by the purple reflection of the lightning. A couple of times I got the same feeling, that of being watched but I could never work out where it was coming from. Not that I had time.

The evening flew by and before I knew it, Liberation was on stage, as the final act. Eloise, Joe, Anna and I jumped to our feet, along with a few other members of the audience. The performance of Chasing the Sunset was the best that I had heard them play and The Swan Nebula, as a follow up, was just as good. The applause was deafening, especially when all of the groups came on stage together to say goodnight. All that was left now was to allow the judges' time to decide on who would win.

Fifteen minutes later, following an impressive performance by the local symphony orchestra, all of the groups were summoned back on stage – and this time the nerves showed in many of the faces. In true talent contest style, the compere thanked and praised them all for their performances, assuring them that they were all winners for their areas. Then he walked over to the judges and collected the results.

He read them, looked back at the judge and then re-read them. Then he walked around the tables and spoke to the judges direct. There was obviously something unusual about the results that he wanted to check but the audience started fidgeting with apprehension. After what felt like many minutes but in reality was probably much less than that, he returned to the stage.

How so many people could keep so quiet? You could have heard a pin drop in that room but in reality all I could focus on was the storm outside and again I failed to hold back a shiver. The lights lit the whole stage once more and the compere walked to centre front.

"Ladies and Gentleman, groups, orchestra and judges, thank you so much for your support throughout this process. Without you it would not have been possible to hold this event and witness the amazing range of talent that our region has to offer. I would like to thank our sponsors, who of course have provided tonight's fantastic prize. Without further delay therefore I can announce the results as follows.

"In third place, winning a session in the Aberfoyle recording studios, come Freedom Fighters from West Bromwich. Congratulations guys." The audience erupted in appreciation, as the group members hugged one another. A few other faces fell, perhaps as they began to understand that, wherever this was going, it was not going to include them.

"In second place and one of my favourite acts for tonight, is Prophets. A highly unusual combination of jazz and folk music – and they win both a studio session and the support act rights to tonight's winner." He paused briefly to allow the applause and congratulations for the folk band.

"Finally, in an unprecedented move, the judges have decided to announce a joint winner to this evening's contest. Both groups will receive a recording contract, agent support and have a UK tour booked, which will be starting at the beginning of next year – that gives the winner just four months to prepare!" The surprise resulted in his final words almost echoing around the room.

"First prize goes to both…Liberation AND Your Reflection."

The room exploded again in appreciation and delight – I found myself cheering, crying and hugging Anna at the same time, overwhelmed with delight that they had won. I turned back to try to catch Ben's eye but although he was looking our way, I could see that the lights were blinding him.

Both bands performed the judges' favourite tracks as the finale, the emotion and joy evident in their respective performances; eventually, after the music finally died the audience started to disperse. I eagerly made my way backstage to help pack and move the equipment, Anna, Joe and Eloise followed.

Ben grabbed me and swung me around, crushing my mouth with his lips, the effect, mingled with his scent sending me weak at the knees again. Letting go, I saw Eloise' smile as she turned to pick up one of the guitar cases. Everyone grabbed what they could and left, carrying them to the car. Ben handed his keys to Will, refusing to let me go so that I could help.

Suddenly we were alone. The bands that had not won, had started their clear up from behind the curtain during the final performances, so most people had already gone.

Lightning lit the auditorium once more and I jumped. Ben held me close, sensing my unease. For a second I buried my head in his chest, breathing his wonderful scent and enjoying the feeling of security. Then finally I looked up and instantly froze. Halfway across the stage, heading right for us was my Father.

"I've had enough of this, you get your filthy mitts off her NOW!" he yelled, his face putrid with rage. I felt, rather than saw, Ben tense at the anger in his voice.

Quickly I glanced around desperate to find an ally that would help us against him. We were well and truly on our own and I had no idea whether Will, Rich or the family would come back to get us, or would be waiting in the car.

Before I could say or do anything, my Father was upon us, grabbing my arm and trying to drag me away. Ben turned and shoved him hard, sending him skidding across the stage towards the pit.

Satisfied that there was enough distance between us, Ben grabbed my hand and we ran, aiming towards the nearest exit. We had only made it down the stage, when thunder erupted again, so loud that it could have been in the room with us, it was followed by a ferocious howl.

I couldn't help it, I skidded to a stop, despite Ben urging me to continue. I knew that sound, I'd heard it many times before in my dreams, I needed to know where it was coming from.

Ben tried to coax me away, to stop me turning but I resisted. I had to understand.

Standing where I had last seen my Father was one of Harbingers of my dreams. The familiar long angular legs, completely bald, with huge claws at both the end of its sinewy arms and webbed feet; it raised its head towards the thunder and howled once more, exhibiting those large sharp teeth, and disgusting drool.

Seeing me standing there, it leapt across the stage, covering most of the distance in one leap. Frozen to the spot I could neither say, nor do, anything; I was completely unable to comprehend the reality before me.

Suddenly Ben was there, in front of me, shielding me with his own body. He was no match for the creature, which swiped him away with its huge claw. Blood pouring from his damaged arm, Ben raced back towards me but the creature got there first. Lifting me high above its head, it went to leap back up on the stage.

A strange, beautiful, harmonic song filled the auditorium, I had never heard anything like it before but somehow it was comforting; the sound was full of life and feeling. Twisting round, it seemed to come from where Ben was racing towards us but that just wasn't possible.

I crashed to the floor, accompanied by another inhuman wail. As I scrabbled to get control of myself, wincing against the bruises forming on my healing wounds, I turned, to see Ben attacking the creature with a piece of wood. Another cry filled the room, just as lightning lit the room, filling it with light. The sickly sweet, metallic scent of blood permeated the air around me and I knew it was coming from Ben.

A flash of movement caught my eye and I instinctively glanced away from the horrific scene in front of me. Sylph-like forms, semi human in shape, but without discernible limbs were entering the room. Across the group their silhouettes shimmered with colour, seeming to represent almost every colour of the rainbow. Perfectly formed, regal heads swayed with the music as they flew swiftly towards us. There were six of them in total and they seemed to be flying towards the fight in front of me. As I watched, one of them broke away from the group and headed in my direction but I was unable to drag my eyes completely away from the scene that was unfolding. The same soulful calls emanated from these wraithlike creatures as they sped towards Ben and it appeared that this was how they were communicating with one another. One sped behind the creature, appearing to form from the body purely for this purpose, long slender arms wrapped around its neck, while the others each captured one of its other limbs. They were so slender, so ethereal; it just didn't seem possible that they would be able to subdue it. Despite their slender appearance and the creature's furious struggles, they lifted and carried the Harbinger away. As they approached the window, the storm seemed to worsen, with streaks of lightning seeming to grab them and carry them forward, melting through the unbroken window and away into the storm.

Stunned I tried to stand, struggling with the injuries that I had sustained in the fall. The remaining creature moved towards me and I shrank back, convinced that it was coming to take me away too.

"No, wait!" I heard Ben's call. I turned, confused, why did he want me to wait? Did he want this being to capture me and take me away too? To my astonishment it appeared as though he spoke to the creature as he continued. "I said wait! She won't recognise you in Seraph form."

I dragged my gaze back to the beautiful creature before me; the one Ben had called a Seraph. It stopped, almost hesitantly and then started to change shape, the silvery glow that emanated from it gradually subsiding as its shape started to morph and then became something almost completely different.

"Leah, it's ok sweetheart, I know it is confusing but everything will be fine." That voice, now, why would my mind play such horrible tricks now?

Despite my fear, I could not haul my eyes away from the changing form in front of me.

"She won't understand and she's hurt, please wait." Ben's voice pleaded, getting weaker with the effort. I forced myself to look at him, blood was soaking through his shirt and there was a large ragged cut to his left cheek.

Despite my concern at his injuries, my eyes raked back to the vision before me. My brain ran in circles, desperately trying to identify the image and make some sense of the events of the last few minutes.

My legs started to give way again and I looked down, to see that my own clothes were also soaked in blood but I couldn't identify the cause. Every inch of me hurt, so that was no help either.

Once again my eyes crept back to the Seraph and I closed them and shook my head. This couldn't be happening, I must be delusional. Forcing myself to open them once more, my brain identified and then finally accepted the shape before me.

It was my mother.

Thunder and lightning circled around me, distorting my vision. I heard a voice screaming for Ben and as I slipped away into oblivion, I realised that the voice was mine.

***

"Leah, sweetheart, everything is ok." Her soft, longed for voice permeated my unconsciousness. My mind stirred in response but I still couldn't make sense of everything before me.

I felt myself being lifted up. Numerous voices, some familiar, others unknown, swirled around and I strained to pick out the two most precious to me. Pain coursed through my body as I struggled to understand what had gone before. Thunder and lightning continued to interrupt the other noises, so loud it felt as though we were right there with it – but I knew that was impossible. Unable to make sense of anything, I slipped further away until I could hear and feel nothing.

Storms

When I awoke, I was surprised to find myself back in my room at the Edwards' house. My shoulder and arm were both heavily bandaged and my left ankle was in a cast but I had absolutely no recollection of having been to a hospital and being treated. Cautiously I looked around the room. It was broad daylight and the clock on the television read 10:47 – but I had no way of knowing which day it was and how long I had been unconscious.

I became aware of the drip that was again connected to the cannula in my hand and looking down at it; I could see the purple edges of the bruising from the night of the finals edging from under the bandages. As the memory flashed through my mind, I shot bolt upright in the bed, crying out with the pain the movement caused.

Where was Ben? How had I got back here?

Seconds later, the door to my room was flung open and Anna came rushing in.

"Leah, you're awake, how are you feeling hun?" She uttered as she rushed in. Her face was drawn and tired and despite her forced pleasantness, I could see that the events of the last few days had taken a significant toll. I wondered how much she actually knew about the events of that evening.

"Ben..?" I asked, unsure of how to word the question, or even begin to express my fear.

She smiled weakly. "Ben is in a pretty bad way right now, he's not here. Don't worry Leah, please. He is safe and being well looked after. My Father will be here soon to explain everything to you. I'm sorry, I must go now but it won't be long, I promise."

With that she scurried back out of the door.

The silence ate away at me, driving me crazy. What did she mean that Ben wasn't here – they'd got all the equipment here for me, so how bad was it? It must be pretty serious; otherwise they would have let Anna tell me, rather than Joe being sent in to explain. I needed to go to him. I needed to see him for myself. My heart beat louder in my ears as I worried, my mind playing games as to just how bad Ben's injuries were, or could be.

As the seconds crawled by, I strained for sounds of someone coming to tell me the truth. Heart aching, I couldn't help wondering whether Ben's injuries had proved to be fatal. Desperately I clung to Anna's words, which still echoed in my mind, "… he's not here." That was still the present tense, wasn't it? Surely she wouldn't have said it like that if he was… I couldn't even think the word "dead."

It felt as though hours had passed by the time my door opened again but the clock told me that it was only ten minutes.

Joe strode into the room. He also looked tired and drawn, as he glanced quickly around the room. Finally he grabbed hold of the chair and dragged it towards the bed, smiling gently as he sat down.

"How are you feeling Leah?" he asked.

"Let's not waste time on me," I shot back, more aggressively than I had intended to. "What is it that you have to explain?"

If he was taken aback, or upset at all by my attitude, it didn't show. Instead he leant forward, his elbows on his knees and rested his chin on his clenched fist.

"Leah, how much have you actually remembered? Of this place before you came back here this time?" he asked.

I looked back at him, confused. What did he mean, this time? Before I could answer he continued.

"Ben has told me a little about what has been happening. Essentially that you've been experiencing bad dreams, which got significantly worse since you returned to Kenilworth. Can you tell me how much you've been able to make sense of, please?" he probed.

"Where is Ben, just how bad is he?" I demanded, deliberately ignoring his questions.

"All in good time Leah, please. Ben was injured quite badly but nothing that won't heal. He's not here right now; he… needs to be looked after elsewhere at the moment. Please Leah, it is very important, what do you remember?" he insisted.

"Remember about what?" I shot back, the frustration evidenced by the tone of my voice. "I've had enough of all of these secrets. I'm sorry, I don't mean to sound ungrateful for everything that you have all done for me but there is obviously something that you are hiding from me. That is despite the fact that it affects me quite significantly. I need an explanation, right now; otherwise I shall talk to whoever will listen until I do get the answers that I need. After everything that happened that night at Symphony Hall, I think I deserve at least that!"

"I can't explain Leah, not everything. There is some of the detail that only you yourself can reveal. I can help you though... help you find the truth, if you'll let me? There is one thing that I need you to promise though, right now Leah? You need to trust me. My job, the whole purpose of my being here right now is to protect you and I can only do that if you are completely honest with me. Can you do that?" he asked.

What choice did I have? The only chance that I stood of finding out what was really going on and understanding the truth, sat in front of me.

I closed my eyes briefly, angry at the lack of options I had available, then, finally I nodded.

"Ok, then this is what we will do." Joe replied. "You will be taken to the place where you be able to learn the truth but in return, you must promise that, from this moment on, you will tell me, in detail, everything that happens, whether it is in a dream or not. It is only by being open with one another that I can ensure your safety, do I have your promise?"

Again I nodded.

"Then I will go and ask Anna to return and help you get changed. Once you are ready, meet myself and Eloise in the living room – okay?"

At my nod, he stood and walked towards the bed. Despite myself I shrank back into the pillows. He took a sterile pack from the bedside cabinet next to the bed and then gently took my hand. The warmth from his touch seeped through me, as he cautiously removed the drip from my hand, replacing it with a small dressing. Without speaking he cleared the debris and left the room, closing the door firmly behind him. Although annoyed at the situation, I knew that I had no other choice in the matter. Resigned to what may come, I gingerly climbed from the bed, determined to get myself ready as much as I could. By the time Anna arrived, I had managed a lot of it. Although unable to shower, I had cleaned myself up reasonably well – I just needed her help pulling my shirt on and, most embarrassingly, doing up my jeans. I'd scraped my hair back with a headband, as I refused to have to ask her to do my hair too.

Once satisfied that I was respectable, Anna opened the door to my room and we made our way down the little corridor and towards the living room. Once more I was struck by the stunning décor of the house. There was not a single thing where the item or splashes of colour were not exactly right. I didn't have time to dwell on it though, I needed to focus on what was about to come. I tried to prepare myself but how do you do that, when you have absolutely no concept about what *is* about to come?

As I entered the living room, I was surprised to see Eloise and Joe already seated, waiting for me,

Anna went and joined them, as though they had known all along that I would agree with Joe's suggestion. They sat in a u-shape, with an empty chair filling the square. As I hobbled towards them Eloise gave me one of her graceful smiles and nodded to the chair. My frustration bubbled again, they had promised to take me to the place where I could finally begin to understand the truth and now they wanted a little chat did they? Despite this annoyance, yet again I was left with little choice. As I perched on the edge of the seat, I saw a single glance pass between them, as Joe went to sit forward. Hesitating slightly he sat back and Eloise began to speak.

Or rather began to sing. As she did so, a shiver ran up my spine. Although in a different key, the song was identical to the one that I had heard that night at Symphony Hall. Despite myself, I turned and scoured the room, looking for something, an instrument or a stereo system, something that could be playing this song – even though I could see for myself that it was coming from Eloise.

As the surreal tune continued, I felt my body begin to relax, gradually getting heavier. Annoyed with my reaction, I forced myself to sit up straighter; there was no way I was going to let my injuries stop me learning the truth now. Eloise continued and despite all of my efforts, I could feel my body succumbing. As hard as I fought against it, it seemed to fight back just as hard. I tried focussing on specific objects in the room but it was as though everything was under the influence of this noise.

I started to pick out specific things, the tiffany lamp, and the regency chair by the side table but at each point that I sought, objects were moving. Not floating, or even flying but moving gradually as though to a pulse. As the pace of the song picked up, so did the movements and I realised that it wasn't just the objects that I was looking at that were vibrating, everything around us was moving, as though in a whirlwind and our seats were the eye of it. Thunder and lightning, seemingly inside the house, accompanied the song as it got louder and louder, building alongside an echo and the combined effect filled the room with sound.

The song reached a crescendo, piercing the accompanying echoes clearly. As it did so, everything else began to subside and settle and as I began to focus suddenly I realised that we were back in the room once again. I'm not sure what I had expected to happen but ending up back in the same place certainly wasn't it. But something was different, as I took in my surroundings once more, there were little things, colours seemed slightly different, tables were in slightly different places – and yet on the surface everything looked the same.

I dragged my eyes back to Eloise, a question forming in my mind but what I saw drove that away. Sitting in her place was the most stunning creature I had ever seen. Don't get me wrong, Eloise, as I knew her was a beautiful lady but this creature was beyond that. Tall, willowy and wraithlike, it seemed to float where she had sat. I must have looked a complete sight, sitting there gazing in awe at her – yet despite the appearance, I knew this being was still actually

Eloise. Dressed in shimmering metallic colours of gold and silver, the glow radiated with sparks of the same colours, making her appear to shimmer in front of me. Her body, although generally still human in overall shape, appeared to have no legs, the gown she wore tapering to a point below where her feet would have been, had they touched the floor. Long wispy arms were gracefully placed beside her as she floated on the chair. Her face, although glowing now like the rest of her, was still somehow the same and those gorgeous eyes shone from within, filling the smile on her face with warmth.

I glanced to her left, first. Joe had also transformed. His appearance was far less wraithlike, more sturdy and striking really and he definitely seemed to retain a more human appearance. Glancing down quickly I could see feet protruding from his trousers and he also appeared to float above, rather than sit on, the seat he had previously occupied. His colours were darker but still metallic – gunmetal, old gold and midnight blue but still he shimmered with the colours. Glancing quickly the other way, I saw that Anna however remained herself, although this was obviously something she had witnessed before, she didn't have the look of shock that I knew must be on my face.

Then Eloise finally spoke.

"Leah, I know this is a lot for you to take in right now but you deserve to know the truth – about yourself and what has happened to you over the course of your lifetime. Your mind has been trying to show you for some time now but consciously you are blocking it and the… medication… that you have been taking has encouraged that." She shook her head slowly. "I wish there was a better way of doing this Leah and I myself am not convinced you are ready for it, I think we should have allowed your injuries to heal first. But you have insisted you are told the truth. This is your final chance to give yourself time to come to terms with what you have already seen, before you know the rest?" The question lingered for a few moments and I shook my head impatiently. How could they expect me to back down now? I had a right to know what was going on and this so-called truth that they kept going on about.

Eloise lowered her head slightly, as though surrendering to what had to be done. Then she lifted her head and held out a long, slender arm. "Come, then Leah, I will show you what you need to know. But the journey must come from you."

I looked at her confused – what did she mean by that? Hesitantly I stood and made my way to her. As my hand met hers, a huge jolt shot through my body. Flashing images shot through my mind, dreams mixed with memories. Instinctively I tried to pull away but I was held fast. Unwanted images from my nightmares appeared, the little girl, the awful creature with the haunting yellow eyes at the back of the car and finally the sight of my mother's body and Dad trying to get me out of the car. Nodding with satisfaction, Eloise gripped harder. "Let yourself go Leah, you must allow yourself to discover the truth," she urged.

Much as I wanted to know, I couldn't bring myself to follow her lead. It felt as though something were tugging at me, trying to drag me back to the detail. I couldn't let go though, I didn't want to go back to that period in my life again, back to the fresh rawness of losing Mom. Again unbidden, the image from Symphony Hall of the transforming Seraph, entered my mind. With a sharp pull I found myself floating, heading towards the image in my mind, with Eloise at my side. Thunder and lightning erupted once more and I finally understood the relevance as the storm drew us to its centre, through the eye of the noise and light, guiding our path forward. Bewildered I turned to ask what the hell was going on but she smiled gently and shook her head and before I could stop it, we were there, watching my unconscious body slip to the floor.

The Seraph turned towards us and acknowledged Eloise with a slight bow. Her sweet, so longed-for voice filled my ears.

"Leah, darling, please don't be scared. I know that this is a lot for you to take in right now but I need to explain and to show you the truth. Are you ready for that?" she asked.

My mind searched for an explanation as to how this was happening but found nothing, because of course there was no rational explanation. I gazed into my Mother's face, a million questions and accusations scorching my mind and simply nodded.

I felt Eloise let go of my arm and panicked. Twisting and turning I sought to catch hold again, convinced that I would float away into the ether and never be able to return to either world without her. At this precise moment in time however, I didn't really want to return. I had found my Mother, who I'd thought was dead for the last five years and there was a big part of me that never wanted to leave her side again.

As I struggled I felt a hand grab hold of me and instinctively I recognised the touch. Turning towards her, I saw the smile and the tears in her eyes and knew that they mirrored my own. Gently she pulled me towards her but instead of resting beside her, I found that we were travelling again. Colours and smells blended into one another as we flew into the storm and I knew I had no chance of recognising where we were.

Until, that was, we came to a standstill.

We were back at the castle, in one of my favourite spots with the huge old tree shielding the area from the worst of the elements and the grass around it continually trying to defy any attempt at cultivation. I looked around, concerned that a member of the public would spot us. How on earth could I explain the appearance of my Mother to another human being? But as I looked at her, I realised that she had transformed, into the familiar body that I loved so much. Unless they knew, anyone watching us right now would simply see a mother and daughter enjoying the ruins together. Or so I thought.

That is, until Mom walked behind the tree, pressing one of the iron support bolts in the ruins, she opened a doorway into the ruin that I had never seen, or at least never noticed before. As we entered I saw a steep flight of stairs descending in a spiral and I followed my mother cautiously, wary both of where we were going and what was about to happen.

Although we passed a few more of the Seraphs, none seemed to either acknowledge or be concerned by our presence and I couldn't help wondering if the image of my mother that I could now see was some kind of projection – so that humans saw the human image and Seraphs saw one of their own. I wasn't going to get that answer quickly though, as we descended further into the darkness.

Finally, she led the way into a small room. Faint daylight streamed through a vent near to the ceiling but it was not big enough to provide the light that filled the room. I looked around, at the light coloured, gothic style chairs and table. Every flat surface had glass globes standing on it, each one containing what I could only assume was a candle of some sort, as the entire ball was filled with golden light.

She gestured to one of the chairs and reluctantly I sat down. The last thing I wanted right now was a simple cosy chat. I needed answers, not platitudes.

"Be patient, Leah, all in good time," came her response. I looked at her in surprise, I could have sworn that her mouth had not moved and yet I'd heard her voice clearly.

"Stop fighting it Leah, you know what's happening." There it was again and this time I knew that she hadn't spoken, I'd been looking directly at her.

"How...what is happening?" I asked, attempting to follow her lead. She smiled at the attempt, despite the fact it had half been thought, the other half said.

"Take it slowly sweetheart, you've a lot of catching up to do. First I need you to drink this, it will help you to relax and access your powers. I shall then take us both on a journey so that you get your questions answered."

Despite everything that had happened and all that I had seen, I instinctively accepted the warm drink that she offered. The scent of herbs filled my nostrils – I could detect rosemary, ginger, wild mint and a few others that I could not name. It was invigorating at the same time as calming. As I sipped, the warmth coursed through me, every nerve was awake and yet I did not feel agitated. Instead I felt alive, more alert than I had ever felt before. I waited, expectantly, anticipating a story that revealed the truth. The reality was completely different.

Truth

I was back at the Castle, the long gravel drive snaking away from me and the car park directly behind me. Although it was night-time, there was sufficient moonlight to ensure that most of what lay before me was visible.

The little girl was crying again, only this time I knew that I didn't need to go looking for her – I could feel the tears streaming down my face.

Thunder and lightning erupted from behind me, despite the fact there were still no clouds around.

"It's alright Leah, just go with it and follow the story. You need to discover the truth." My Mom's voice pierced my mind again.

Instinctively I knew I had to find him, despite everything that had happened to the nineteen year old me, the ten year old standing here was lost and needed that father figure to make her safe. I turned this way and that, eyes scouring the area, looking for his familiar face. There was no sign of anyone. I ran down the path, taking the right hand fork towards the little car park – perhaps I'd got it wrong and we'd parked there, not the main car park. As I ran, tears still streaming, the roar started. Mixed with the sound of thunder it was the most terrifying sound that my little ears had ever heard. I ran faster and faster, until I was almost falling over with the pace but still that sound got louder.

I practically jumped over the little stile that led to the other car park. As I turned the corner, I saw a familiar shape ahead of me.

"Daddy!" I screamed running towards him.

The man turned at the sound of my voice, a huge smile of relief on his face but as he focussed that smile froze into panic.

"Run, Leah, run, come on darling you can do it!" Gasping for breath, I sped towards him. The roar behind me was getting louder and louder; then suddenly another sound joined it – the sound of a car. Squealing tyres could be heard and then a dark coloured sedan span round the corner to the car park entrance and I finally recognised the car as our own, just as I reached him.

"Leah, you have to listen to me, you're in real danger," he said.

I jumped, glancing towards his shadowy figure beside me. I loved this man with all of my little heart. Not only was he my Father, he was also our Guardian, charged with keeping my Mother and now myself, safe. The rest of the world we lived in thought he was my Father. Even I thought of him just as Daddy, most of the time. It was only times like this that I remembered his other role, the one that had got him and my mother into so much trouble.

I shook my head in confusion. I was with him now, so how could I be in any danger? It felt so safe. I sensed his arm wrap around my waist, holding me tight against him, protecting me. Despite my fear, my body warmed to his touch, encouraging me to snuggle in even closer.

The noise grew closer; I still couldn't quite work out what it was, although every nerve in me screamed of the danger. It was so loud now that I couldn't make out where it was coming from.

His arm suddenly tightened around me. Despite the noise and everything else, I felt as though I could stay here forever and always be kept safe.

Suddenly the car pulled alongside us.

"Get in!" screamed the driver. He grabbed my arm and before I knew it we were in the back of the car and he was struggling to get my seatbelt on. I snatched it off him as he dove into the seat beside me. "Go!" he yelled. The car accelerated away, filling with the scorching smell of stressed rubber.

He turned towards me and grabbing my shoulders with both hands he pulled me in close to him. "Thank God you're safe," he said, holding me tight against him and burying his head in my hair.

Abruptly, there was a huge crash from somewhere right alongside the car and I spun to look out of the rear view window. "Step on it!" he bellowed, reaching across me to grab something. A pair of luminous yellow eyes stared at me from shadows at the back of the car.

I cringed and turned back, in time to see Daddy throwing something through the open window. It was one of the strange glowing balls like I'd seen in my mother's room and it exploded into millions of tiny shards of light as it landed. Judging by the howl that came from the side of the road it had injured something and as I looked back into the remaining light as it faded, I realised it was another of the Harbingers. How many of them were there, I wondered and did he have another for the one still hanging off the back of the car?

There was another crash and suddenly the yellow eyes were at the car window. I found myself trying to hide in the seat of the car, pushing as far away from the window as I could. The eyes continued to stare at me for what seemed like an age, before Daddy launched another ball through the window, another explosion of light and it was gone.

We sped away, through the storm. My mother glanced in the rear view mirror and smiled reassuringly at me, before turning her look to the man beside me. The look that passed between them was pure love.

***

I felt my body begin to stir, cramping in the chair in my mother's room.

"It's okay, Leah, let the memory run, there is more for you to see yet. Here, drink some more," she urged. Obediently, just as I always had when I was a child, I followed her instructions.

Once more I felt my body grow heavy and start to drift. This time however I was alone as I drifted back towards the castle. As I glanced down, I could tell that this was a completely different period in time – I was much older. Looking at my favourite sparkly pumps, I could tell that I was now about fourteen. I arrived back in the car, with the scorched rubber smell and squealing tyres accompanying the sound of the brakes.

The car door slammed behind me. Long fleshless claws reached through the broken window scratching at my arm as it tried to grab me and pull me away. It uttered a horrendous yowl as the car accelerated away, throwing it onto the pathway. As I watched in horror, it leapt to its feet and tore after us, quickly joined by another slightly smaller Harbinger.

"Leah it will be ok, we just need to get you away from here and then we will all be fine," my mother said as she smiled at me through the mirror.

"Watch out," Daddy's voice came from beside me as he grabbed me and held me tight. I heard the squealing of brakes, the scrabbling of tyres as they fought to come to a standstill and a scream. I was suddenly flying through mid-air, crashing into the seat in front of me. I watched my Father continue the journey forward; between the two front seats of the car and a few seconds later I heard glass shattering, just as I began to ricochet back onto the rear seat of the car with a huge jolt. Grinding metal complained as it was forced to an instant stop and my head bounced off the headrest of the seat. Finally the crescendo of noise ceased and I was left with nothing but silence. Absolute silence.

As I struggled to make sense of what had just happened, the door of the car was ripped open and a long morbid brown arm, with extended claws, reached in, grabbing me and started to drag me out of the car, I struggled and screamed for both of my parents but as my eyes focussed on their bodies I could see that both were dead.

I fought and struggled as hard as I could. Kicking and screaming, even trying to bite the creature, although his skin was more like armour. Thunder and lightning erupted around us once more as he dragged me out of the car and over towards the trees. As I continued to struggle he lifted his head to the sky and uttered that lifeless howl three times. An echo of howls followed and before I knew it, two more creatures appeared from the trees. They loped towards us, chuntering between themselves and my captor. Despite my kicking and struggling, each took one of my legs and before I knew it I had been carried into the trees.

I struggled and struggled using every ounce of strength I could muster but with these beings it was no use, not that the knowledge stopped me trying.

My Father's voice echoed in my ears from over the years. "The Harbingers must never take you Leah, if your powers were to cross over between the Worlds, the balance of power would shift and things would start to descend into chaos – which, of course, is just what Nilameth wants." With the memory piercing my mind I struggled even harder. The thunder was getting louder and it felt as though I was being carried right into the storm, as the wind developed further and further, until it whipped my breath away from me. I craned my neck around, trying desperately to see where we were going and almost wished that I hadn't. We were heading directly towards what appeared to be the eye of the storm. Leaves and litter swirled around, like the pictures I'd seen of a tornado and these creatures were loping directly into it. Terrified I continued my fight but this time I must have caught a nerve because the creature carrying me paused briefly. Bringing his clawed hand, palm first down sharply, he struck me across the side of my head. Flashing lights burst in my eyelids as the pain seared from the point of impact and then everything went black.

***

Somehow, although I could feel everything as we travelled through that storm; I knew that the child me had been unconscious. I could hear the continuous chuntering between them as they communicated, although I had no idea what was being said.

Suddenly everything was calm again. There were no sounds of wind, or flashes of lightning. All that was left were the retreating rumbles of thunder.

I felt myself being placed gently down and the smell of perfume and talc made me think that I was in my own room. How could that be? Someone leant over me and kissed me very gently on my forehead. I recognised the smell instantly but that wasn't possible, either. As footsteps retreated towards the door, I cautiously opened my eyes.

A familiar figure was about to leave the room. Almost as though he knew, he turned and looked at me. The eyes, the face and the body… they all belonged to Daddy. The little girl inside me smiled at him, relieved that he was still there. I knew that it wasn't really him – the injuries he had suffered in the crash were too severe, my adult mind recognised that he would have been unable to survive those injuries – besides, this version bore none of the scars.

"Here you go sweetheart, the Doctor has left this medicine for you to take – have one now. You were absolutely devastated when the Police came with the news, these will help you sleep for a few days until you get used to it. I'm sorry darling; your Mom isn't coming back." There was a hard yellow glint hidden in the depths of his eyes as he spoke and suddenly I realised the truth. This father figure before me was the creature that had carried me into the storm.

***

There was no gradual stirring this time. I shot upright in the chair in my Mother's room, heart racing, scouring the room until I found her again.

As she caught my eyes, she smiled again and then spoke, filling the gaps in what I had just seen, ensuring that my understanding was true.

"You are right, darling, in what you have seen. That night, the night Daddy and I lost our mortal shells; *you* were taken by the Harbingers. They took you to Earos, the parallel dimension to Earth – and your captor shifted to the image of your father. Just as he had always warned you, Nilameth's agents are extremely dangerous and they are very clever at shape shifting. The tablets he was giving you in those early days enabled him to reprogram your memory – so, for a while at least, you believed that he was your Father and that not only had just I died that night in the accident but that I had been travelling alone."

"What *they* don't know, or didn't until now, is that you are not *just* a Seraph. Your Father is, or was, a Shear blood." She saw my flinch and the question forming – or had she read the question as it shaped in my mind?

"Yes, he was both your Father as well as our Guardian, as you always knew, although he was cast out from the Shears because we fell in love. It is not permitted for a Guardian, let alone a Shear, to fall in love with their charge, despite their incredible capacity for love. We raised you as a couple here on Earth but with him as your Guardian, because that's how the Savant insisted. If we had disagreed, they would have forced us apart and that would have been devastating. So we lived as a family on Earth but as a Guardian and his charges to the rest of the worlds, until the Harbingers found us. At first, they were just trying to kill us – *they* are one of the Sprite races. Those that try to stop the work of the Seraphs in supporting the Savant. I don't know what gave it away but when they realised the truth, that first time they tried to get us, their plans changed and that final time, the plan was always to take *you*."

She smiled gently at me and then walked across the room. For the first time since I had seen her again, she wrapped her arms around me as I wept. Tears that had refused to come when I had first lost her now came pouring out, in great dry racking sobs, as though I had only just discovered her loss. These were for my Father though, the man I grew up with, loving as only a little girl can love her father, now knowing that he had died to save me. I cried for what had happened to him, for the lost years and for the way I had come to hate him recently – when it hadn't been him at all.

She held me tight, gently wiping my tears away, cradling my head against her shoulder as she had done so many times in my life. I could hear her thoughts, her own grief – less recent than my own but just as raw, eating away at her. I read her struggles to contain that loss, in order that she could comfort her child and also realised the pain she had endured during our separation.

As my tears subsided, I managed to control my breathing. "How did you survive, when Daddy didn't?" I asked.

"I survived, because I am not pure Seraph. Each dimension has its own special race and I am the result of a relationship between the Epoch voyager race of Earos and a Guardian. This gave me a form of immortality, in my Seraph form at least. As a result, the special… tools… that the Harbingers were given to bring to Earth to capture you did not result in my ultimate death, although I was unfortunately unable to stop them taking you."

I shook my head slowly, trying to take everything in.

"Leah, your Father isn't dead, at least, not in the sense you believe, in terms of being gone forever," she continued. "As a Guardian, he also is immortal. They occupy mortal shells, those of precious young people that have passed before their time and a shell is usually assigned that it is in its late teens or early twenties. That way they can mature in that shell and be assigned charges for a significant period. They can pass as a human for a number of years without arousing any suspicions. Then when it reaches old age, it passes and the Guardian moves on to the next available shell. As a punishment though, for falling in love with me and for becoming your Father, he is being kept in… storage… until such time as the Savant believe he can be released."

Again I could read the pain and distress this caused her. I needed to understand more, why their relationship was so frowned upon. But there was another more important question I wanted to ask.

"Yes, Leah, you are right. Ben is a Shear Guardian, just like your Father. In fact they are descendant from the same line. That is why Joe and Eloise believe that you can never be together. Although your blood is purer than my own, you are still not considered appropriate as a partner. The Savant forbids it."

As she spoke those final words her voice broke and she held me to her again. She was unable to hide the turmoil of pain and anger in her mind and I knew that she would also be able to read it in my own. Eventually she tenderly pushed me away.

"Leah, it's time for you to go back – not to the cottage but to what is now your home." I began to argue – after everything that had happened and I had just seen, I needed to be close to her. She just shook her head.

"It's ok sweetheart, I will always be with you, here and here." She said gently touching my temple and then my heart. "Just as I have tried to remain with you throughout the last few years, although I have been unable to protect you as I should. All you need to do is send your thoughts to me and I will come but you need to go back now to where Joe and Eloise can keep you safe."

With that she stood and returned to the little table. Moving swiftly she mixed another drink, this time the smell permeated the room. Eucalyptus and lime filled my lungs even before I had to drink it. Every sinew in my body wanted to reject the drink but the look in her eyes told me it was futile.

Obediently, I took the mixture and drank it all.

Dreams

When I awoke, I was back in the Edwards'
bedroom, lying in my bed. My shoulder and arm
were still heavily bandaged and my left ankle
remained in the cast. Cautiously I looked around the
room. It was broad daylight and the clock on the
television read 10:57 – seemingly just ten minutes
after I had last awoke. I had no way of knowing
which day it was and how long I had been
unconscious.

Instinctively I looked down at my bruised
hand, expecting to see the drip there once more but it
wasn't there. As the thought flashed through my
mind, I shot bolt upright in the bed, crying out with
the pain the movement caused. Where was my
Mother? How had I got back here?

Seconds later, the door to my room was flung
open and Anna came rushing in.

"Leah, you're finally awake, how are you
feeling hun?" She uttered as she rushed in. Her face
was still drawn and tired and despite her forced
pleasantness, I could see recent events had taken

their toll. I wondered how much they actually knew about my discoveries.

"I'll just go and get Joe – he can explain everything to you," she said, hurrying back towards the door, then she stopped and turned back. "Ben isn't here, he's being taken care of... elsewhere... until he is fully recovered."

Her words echoed in my mind as she left. This was just too bizarre; it was as if my last journey had yet to happen. As I went to sit back against the pillows I winced, looking down at my other hand, I saw the needle from the drip being held by a simple white plaster.

Return to the Beginning

"Leah, Leah, come back, you need to come back, NOW." Her voice broke through my consciousness, invading the control I had maintained over my presence in the past. The undercurrent of panic I the voice registered and reluctantly I released my past body, allowing myself to return to my prone position under the tree.

It didn't matter how many times I did this, I hadn't yet mastered the disorientation that resulted from returning to the present. At least normally I had reached the end of my journey and therefore the episode closed before I travelled. This time was different.

Again the urgency I'd heard in her voice registered and I pulled myself together, allowing my body to adjust to my presence once more and my eyes come into focus. As they did, the change in the weather caught my attention.

The sky had turned a deep purple and lightning flashed across my sight. I glanced towards her in trepidation, to see the look of abject horror on her face. From behind me came that inhuman, guttural growl that I now recognised so easily and without speaking I leapt towards her, grabbing her and spinning her behind me as I turned towards it.

The Harbinger grinned as it looked at me, cackling at the fact it had found me unprepared but it didn't know that I had come into my full powers.

Slowly and carefully I watched as it started to move towards me, once again amazed at the control I had over the passing of time. Making sure she was safe, I opened my mind calling silently for help from the other Shear and I heard their swift response. Satisfied that help was on its way, I allowed the Harbinger to come even closer, permitting it to believe that this time it had won.

As it got to within striking distance, I braced myself, preparing for a blow from one of those long clawed limbs. As it raised its arm, the sky filled with the song of my kind and I watched with more pleasure than I should, as my family swept down and dragged him away, writhing and yowling in protest. Satisfied that we were once again safe I turned back.

Her eyes were wide with pride and wonder. "Your Father would be so proud of you, how I wish he was here to see what you have become." Tears glittered as she watched me.

"Come on, Mom, you know I can't change that, no matter how much I want to. All I can do is try my best to fulfil the future I was meant to have, that he died to protect." Wrapping my arm around her shoulder, we walked together back into our little cottage, our refuge, our home.

Please bear with me why I indulge in thanking a few people, for their friendship, support and advice:

Ken Dawson – Creative Covers

Dr. Sam Dogra

K A Jack

Will Macmillan Jones

Lindsey J Parsons

AFE Smith

Lisa L Wiedmeier

The Alliance of World-builders,
www.theallianceofworldbuilders.weebly.com